OPERATION: LONDON

S-SQUAD BOOK 13

WILLIAM MEIKLE

SEVERED PRESS
HOBART TASMANIA

OPERATION: LONDON

- WIGGO -

"Fuck me, Cap. When you said it was a shite assignment I didnae think you meant it literally."

Wiggo looked down into the sewer below the manhole. He didn't bend for a closer look; the smell of the hot air that rose up was rank enough to floor an incontinent elephant.

"London, eh? About what I expected. So who did we piss off this time?"

Captain John Banks stood off to one side with a cigarette stuck between his teeth, and when he spoke he barely moved his lips.

"We've got the Minister to thank for this one, lads. They've been having a spot of bother here and somebody in Westminster said there was nothing that could be done. Our man, after a few bevvies in the Member's Bar, piped up that he had a team who could get anything done. They dared him to put his money where his mouth was, so here we are."

"So we get covered in shite just because some politician got pished and couldnae keep his mouth shut?"

"Same as it ever was, Wiggo," Banks replied. "It's no' as if it's the first time."

Wiggo spat down into the hole.

"And this problem. It's in the nature of what, exactly?"

"Missing people," Banks replied. "At first it was the homeless and nobody seemed too bothered

1

when they weren't on the streets anymore, but two days ago a stockbroker and her man disappeared right about here, and money talks."

Right about here was in Farringdon Road a hundred yards north of Blackfriars. Wiggo could see two pubs from where they stood. They looked much more inviting than what was below them.

"And the brass think they're doon there?"

"Well, they've looked everywhere else," Banks said and laughed. "Come on, Wiggo. A wee bit of shite's never bothered you before."

Davies and Wilkins were on the other side of the manhole, climbing into yellow, heavy rubber one-piece suits. Wiggo jerked a thumb in their direction.

"Looks like we're preparing for more than a wee bit," he said, and Banks laughed again.

Ten minutes later they were all suited up. They were going down with two London council workers as guides who showed them how to operate the helmet lights, respiratory gear and radios. Wiggo felt naked without his flak jacket and rifle.

"So what do we use if we do find something? Harsh language?"

One of the council workers laughed. Wiggo realized they were on the same wavelength when he replied in a broad East London accent.

"I like to keep this nearby for close encounters."

Unlike the rest of them, the council man carried a small portable fire extinguisher along with his air tank.

"Have you ever had to use it?" Wiggo asked as they prepared to descend.

"Once, on a rat," the man replied. "The bloody thing was the size of a pony."

Wiggo eyed the manhole with even more trepidation than previously as he put on his helmet and goggles.

They went down in single file, the squad in between the two council workers, ten feet down the steel rungs of a corroded ladder. Wiggo had worried that they'd be confined in a narrow dark corridor but they came down into a brickwork tunnel almost as wide as the road above. They stood on a raised walkway to one side of where a river of sewage flowed sluggishly away toward the south. With the respirator on and the goggles over his eyes there was only the faintest trace of the stench, and his helmet light lit up the dry walkway stretching away in both directions.

"Well, this isnae so bad," Wiggo said, then realized he was live on radio when the older of the two guides spoke up in his ear.

"Not yet," he said, and chuckled. The older man led them away from under the manhole.

The smell immediately got worse, even through the respirator.

The man in front halted them after fifty meters and called the other council man forward. They were pointing their lights into a side tunnel and were having an animated conversation between themselves. Wiggo stepped forward.

"Have you found something?"

"Just a little fatberg," the younger of them said. "We'll make a note and get back to it."

Wiggo looked up the tunnel. It was blocked across the whole circumference with what looked to be a grey mass of damp soap. When he looked closer, he saw there were things embedded in it. He stopped looking closer.

"Is that what I think it is?"

"Probably. Sanitary towels, wet wipes, shit, condoms, cotton buds, chunks of McDonald's and KFC and good old fashioned grease. They all get caught in eddies in the current and start to accumulate and mash together. Saponification is the posh name for it. Then they grow until they clog up the system. They're a bloody nuisance."

Wiggo looked at how the mass clogged the entire tunnel, some eight feet in diameter.

"And you say this is a wee one?"

"Hell, yeah. They dug one out of Whitechapel a few years back that was quarter of a mile long and weighed a hundred and thirty tons."

"I'm glad we're not in Whitechapel."

"That makes two of us, man."

Having made his notes on his phone, the older man led them off again. It was still dry underfoot.

"It's a lot cleaner than I expected. I thought there would be rats."

"Usually there are," the man in the lead said. "Packs of the wee buggers...and some not so wee. But they've mostly buggered off in recent months. Not that I'm complaining, like. The men upstairs think the Covid got them."

"Thank fuck for small mercies," Wiggo muttered.

"Amen to that," the man at the rear replied.

They moved deeper in silence for several minutes until they were all stopped by a whispered oath from the supervisor in front.

"Fuck me sideways," he said, little more than a whisper. When the man stepped aside to let his fellow worker pass, Wiggo got a good view of the scene ahead. He agreed with the first man's comment.

Once, in Africa, Wiggo had seen what was left of a wildebeest after a pride of lions was through with it. The bones then had all been picked and licked clean. The makeshift ossuary that lay before them in the sewer was full of bones that were cleaner still, gleaming, almost polished. They were strewn all across the width of the sewer, jumbled and piled in mounds. Things glittered among the rib cages and skulls; mobile phones, earrings, jewelry, watches and spectacles, only plastic and metal remaining where flesh had been stripped. At a guess, Wiggo thought they were looking at what was left of thirty, maybe even forty, people, adults and children all piled together in death.

"What the fuck happened here?" the supervisor whispered.

"You're the expert. You tell us," Wiggo replied.

"I've never seen anything like it," the other worker said. "And I don't want to ever again. I'm out of here."

"That sounds like a plan," Captain Banks said. "We need to get a forensics team in here right sharpish before this lot gets washed away."

"Never mind that," the supervisor said. "What the fuck did this?"

Wiggo spoke slowly, calmly, hearing the panic in the man's voice.

"As the Cap says, forensics is what's needed. They'll get to the bottom of it. Let's just get you lads back up top; things will look better under the sun."

Wiggo had been partially right; things looked slightly better back up top, but there was little sun. A gray pallor hung over the city and a light drizzle was falling. The captain was making a quick report to the ministry men on site and there was a flurry of activity among the suits. Wiggo had moved off to one side to shuck himself out of the protective gear and was leaning on one of the crowd-control barriers when someone spoke right behind him.

"It's back, isn't it?"

Wiggo already guessed it was an old man before he turned, and saw it was a *really* old man, an almost dwarfish figure bent by age, leaning heavily on a stout cane. But the eyes were vivid blue, clear and almost wild as he looked Wiggo in the eye and continued.

"I thought it might be Oxford again. All these years I've been watching Oxford. But here it is, right under my feet. It's all my fault, and I'm too bloody old now to do anything about it. You've got to do something, son. You've got to do it for me, and them as went before me."

"Another nutter," Wiggo thought, but didn't say. He'd learned a long time ago it was better to play nice with civilians rather than try to interact meaningfully with them. He was half turning away even as he replied.

"Don't fret, granddad, we're on the case."

"Don't you dare patronize me, son," the old man said, his voice stronger, more forceful than before. It was a voice Wiggo recognised, one used to command. He guessed this old lad had been in service at one time, and not in the lower ranks either. For a second Wiggo thought he was about to get a stout whack on the head from the cane as his guess was confirmed. "I served before you were born. And I know how the bureaucracy works. They'll do sod all until it's too late, then blame you for it. It's happened before and it'll happen again. Just like he said it would."

Wiggo was having trouble following the old man's train of thought; he was too busy watching the cane, which was still being waved in front of his face.

"He? Who's he?"

The old man kept going as if he hadn't heard.

"You need to read this," he said. He took a small notebook out of his jacket pocket and thrust it at Wiggo. Taken by surprise, Wiggo had it in his hand without thinking, and the old man scuttled back so that Wiggo couldn't return it. "He wrote it as a warning. Just read it," he said. "It'll explain everything. You'll be able to find me if you need to find me. But read it. It's important."

Wiggo looked down at the notebook, looked up again, and the old man had melted away into the crowd. Wiggo shrugged, put the notebook into a pocket of his jacket, and promptly forgot about it as Banks called them over for a debrief.

The next few hours were a case of hurry up and wait. Forensics teams arrived and went down into the sewer while the squad was kept on alert in case of emergencies. None came; eventually bones began to be lifted up and out to be spirited away out of view of the myriad of cameras and reporters that lined the control barriers.

Wiggo kept an eye out for the old man but never saw him again, and didn't think about him after that till later that night when they were finally stood down for the day. The forensics teams were going to have a full night of it down in the dark but a backup squad from Kent had the night shift, while the S-Squad were sent back to their hotel.

They were billeted up on Euston Road. It wasn't a five star establishment by any means, but it had beds and it had a bar and that was enough for Wiggo. He had a quick wash and shave and headed for a pint. He arrived in the bar before any of the others. When he was paying for the beer, he felt the weight of the notebook in his pocket and, to fight off the urge for a smoke, took it out and began to read. He was soon lost, somewhere in Oxfordshire in the 1950s.

-THEN-

The trouble started at 6:00pm on a quiet Thursday afternoon and at first it was so small that it was hardly noticed. The summer of '56 had been a hot one so far and was showing no signs of relenting. I had gone outside in search of some escape from the overpowering sense of being slowly boiled in my tin-roofed office. I tried standing under one of the few trees in the shade while smoking down one of my Capstan's but what little wind there was felt too dry, too hot—and the thought of returning to the oven that enclosed my desk was too much to bear. I took a slow, laborious walk over to the only place I knew might give me some respite.

The Rocket Research Group's main laboratory was usually the coolest place in the facility, having the benefit of some new-fangled air conditioning from our American chums. I had sought some solace there just the previous day so I knew a couple of minutes inside would rejuvenate me—for a time at least. When I entered, I saw that young George Thornton was the only other member of staff present and his whole attention was on something under his microscope lens.

"What have you got there, lad?" I asked.

"I don't rightly know, Prof," he said. "I was just about to come and fetch you to have a look. It's a sample we got from the high altitude balloon flight—some top layer stratospheric stuff. I know there's not supposed to be anything alive up there—but this sure looks like life to me."

He motioned me over to take a look.

"Just five minutes ago it was only a spore—I took it for a pollen grain at first. But either the heat or the water on the slide have woken it up—and I've no idea what it is."

I bent over the scope and looked down—it certainly had been a spore at one point—one with a rough, almost hairy outer coat, long fine tendrils that wafted to and fro on the tiny currents caused by the light stage's heat on the fluid under the slide. But now the spore had split and it had a long swollen finger of protoplasm escaping from the right hand edge at about three o'clock as I looked at it. Even as I watched it swelled and oozed further across the field of view. It was full of vivid colors—greens and blues and gold-and it almost seemed to twinkle in the harsh light. It was escaping from the spore so fast that it filled my field of view completely in a matter of seconds and I had to reduce the magnification twice to keep track of the growth.

"It's certainly making itself at home," I said. "Is there just the one of these spores or are there more?"

George shrugged.

"It came from a scraping I took from the bottom of the sample jar—there was a coating, like a hard crust on the outside of the jar when we brought the balloon down."

"And where's the jar now?"

George stood and bent under the desk.

"Down here in the refrigerator—I thought it for the best, what with the heat and all."

He opened the fridge door—and the contents, what was left of them, spilled—or rather, oozed out at his feet. There were Petri dishes, glass sample jars, distilled water bottles and what looked like the remains of a jam sandwich, some of it partially melted, digested, inside what looked like a clear, almost transparent, gelatinous ooze. More of it was already dripping down onto the wooden floor, sending long fat fingers creeping toward George's toes. I saw with some dismay that the seals of the door of the fridge itself had also been partially dissolved—whatever this was, it was voracious.

And it was clearly growing.

Suddenly I was thinking of infection and contagion.

"Don't think—just go. Get out," I said to George. "Now. Hit the sprinklers and flush the system, while we still can."

I followed the lad out of the lab and we both hit the sprinkler button at the same time. A wash of hydrochloric acid came from the showerhead in the ceiling, sending a fine spray through the whole room. We watched the gelatinous ooze as pustules bubbled and popped across its surface. It pulled itself into a tighter clump, almost the size of a football, obviously a defensive maneuver, but not enough to save it as the acid fell and, slowly but surely, dissolved it until it was little more than a puddle on the floor by the fridge. A haze rose over the remains, an oily residue that danced in rainbow colors before falling back into the spilled ooze.

Beyond the window the laboratory fell quiet.

"That was too close," I said once I was sure it was dead. I turned to George—he looked pale, almost ashen. "What's the matter lad—did you get any of that stuff on you?"

"No, Professor," he said. "It's not that—it's just that, when I got the sample jar from the balloon this morning, I saw there was more of that crusty stuff on the surface of the balloon itself—a lot more.

The balloon was one of the focal points of our research—our main tool for investigating the realms into which we intended at some point to launch our first test rocket. Anything that might cause a problem for the balloon was going to cause problems—big ones—for the whole unit. George knew that as well as I did and was out of the door first and beat me to the shed where we kept the kit. He stopped and stood at the door until I approached.

"What do we do if...?" he started, but didn't finish, for neither of us had a ready answer at hand. I stepped past him and opened the door.

This time it was me who had to step back quickly. There was more of the ooze here—much more of it-covering the whole floor of the large storage shed. All that remained of our massive high altitude balloon—so big it normally took six of us to get it out of the shed to prepare it for flight—were a few fragments—already dissolving in a mass of seething protoplasm.

"Fetch some acid, lad," I shouted. The ooze somehow seemed to sense an escape route and surged toward me, forcing me to slam the door hard on it. I remembered the fridge, and I wondered how long it would be before it melted its way through the wood itself.

George hadn't moved. He was staring at the door. I took him by the shoulders and shook him, hard.

"Acid, Thornton. We need it now."

The lad finally came to his senses.

"How much should I get?"

"All of it," I replied, rather too sharply, and then had to stand back. The bottom of the door had gone soft and saggy, threatening to drip. "And best be quick about it. It looks like we don't have much time here."

George left at a run. Other members of our team were, by now, beginning to become aware that something was going on and came out of their huts to investigate. It started to get crowded around the shed door. I sent a couple of the faster lads after George with orders to help him out but I was beginning to wonder whether they'd be on time—or whether we even had enough acid on the facility to cope with what was clearly a rather large menace.

We could all hear groaning and screeching from inside the shed. The structure lurched heavily to one side and the roof fell in with a crash, the door falling inward to join it. A mass of ooze slumped over the rubble then seemed to fall in on itself with a moist slither, then disappeared from view.

I saw the reason as I stepped gingerly forward— the floor, the roof, the door, the balloon and the slime itself, everything had all fallen through the floor of the shed. I had to step closer still to look down into the resulting hole and my sense of foreboding got stronger still—there had been a drain in the center of the shed, which was what had collapsed.

Somewhere, far below, I heard a deep, moist gurgling.

Whatever the stuff was, it was now in the sewer system under our base.

-WIGGO-

Wiggo had been a soldier too long to believe in coincidences. According to the notebook something voracious had got into a sewer in the fifties. The fact that Wiggo had just come out of a sewer when he got the notebook was too much on the nose to be dismissed. When the captain and the others arrived, more beers were bought. Wiggo told them all of his encounter at the barricade. He showed Captain Banks the notebook.

"I thought it was just another random nutter, as you do," Wiggo said. "But after reading this, I'm starting to wonder."

He gave them a summary of what he'd read so far, and Banks agreed with his assessment.

"You'd better read the rest, Sarge," he said. "And right now. It might be nothing, but it might be what we need to figure out what the fuck is going on around here."

But any thought of reading went on the back burner within seconds. The captain got a Code Red call and seconds later, just long enough for Wiggo to down the rest of his beer, they were up and away heading for their supply truck to get kitted up. It moved out as soon as they got inside.

While they were getting prepped the cap brought them up to speed.

"They're still dealing with that shit we found earlier," he said. "But there's been another boneyard found. A fresher one, near High Holborn tube station. They've got another forensics team inbound, but they're getting lary about this, whatever it is. They want backup with them, so we're up."

They suited up with flak jackets, radios, rifles, handguns and stun grenades.

"No wee flame throwers?" Wiggo asked.

Banks smiled.

"They're on order. A couple of hours out so we cannae wait. Just don't get dead in the meantime."

The truck took them down towards Holborn. As they got close to their destination they had to criss-cross through back streets; the main thoroughfares were completely clogged with horn-blaring cars and buses. They discovered the reason when their driver brought them to the intersection of High Holborn and New Oxford Street. The police were in the process of cordoning off the area and traffic was at a standstill in all directions. They made it through just as the last entrance to the junction was barricaded up. Gawkers, reporters and curious commuters were already building up around the perimeter as the squad got out the truck.

Wiggo spotted the same two workmen they'd gone down with earlier, standing in the road above a manhole, having a smoke. The younger one looked pale, almost green around the gills.

"That bad, lads?" he said, and got a nod in reply.

"It's worse," the older man said, grinding out his cigarette. "There's fresh ones this time, if you catch my drift. And something else too; you'll see for yourself when you go down."

Wiggo didn't have long to wait. The captain called the squad together to stand over the manhole.

"I've been told we don't need the hazard suits, for now at least, so thank Christ for small mercies. We'll take the hard hats and helmet lights though, and we go in ahead of the forensics lads. No heroics. We go slow and easy. Don't disturb anything at the scene or the head boffin will have your arse in a sling. Wiggo, you take point."

Wiggo took a long breath of fresh air then headed down the open manhole.

His headlight showed only brickwork at first when he reached bottom but on turning ninety degrees he saw the high arch of the sewer heading away north and south. He wondered which way to go then smelled it, a sickly odor wafting up from his left. He followed his nose and went south. He didn't have to go far.

The workman had been right; this was much worse. Bodies, a score or more, lay in a pile at the intersection where two sewer lines met. Some of them were picked clean as before but others still had some flesh on their bones, although from the quick look Wiggo gave them they looked to have been melted, or partially digested. The beers he'd had earlier went sour in his stomach and he turned away from the sight, holding down a reflex to let it come up and out.

The rest of the squad were coming up behind him so he moved away, circling the remains, giving them as wide a berth as he was able. When he reached the far side, he discovered the *something else* the workman had referred to.

"Hey, Cap. You need to see this," he called out.

Captain Banks came over to join him. They both swung their head-lights south. The sewer looked to have collapsed into itself, or been forced in. A hole, or rather a steeply sloping tunnel some ten feet in diameter, led away from their feet down into blackness. The smooth walls glistened and shimmered giving off an oily rainbow aurora.

"The same phenomena is mentioned in the notebook I got from the auld lad," Wiggo said. "I think we're after the same thing they let loose in the fifties."

"Let's not jump to conclusions," Banks said. "That's nearly seventy years ago. If it's the same thing, where the fuck has it been?"

Wiggo pointed to the hole.

"I'm guessing it's been down there. Growing. In fact, I'd bet my pension on it."

"Aye? Well I'm no' daft enough to take you up on that. When you get a chance, read the rest of the notebook. We might ken a bit more by then."

By this time the forensics team members were filling the intersection. The squad took positions at intervals around the perimeter, with Wiggo deployed at the mouth of the glistening tunnel, looking down into the dark and hoping to hell that nothing was looking back up at him.

He wasn't an engineer by any means but it was obvious that the tunnel wasn't man made. It hadn't been drilled, didn't look to have been excavated by any mechanical means. Like some of the remains behind him the walls appeared to have been melted first then solidified afterwards leaving only an oily glistening residue behind. There was a puddle of said residue at his feet, and Wiggo was careful not to tread in it.

Once again it was time to wait while the forensics team meticulously picked over the site then, eventually, began the slow process of transporting the remains back to the surface. Some hours passed and Wiggo noticed a dimming of all their headlights as the batteries began to run low. He was about to bring it to the captain's attention when their radios all squawked simultaneously.

"Code Red. Code Red. Major incident in High Holborn tube station."

"That's just across the road," the captain said. "Wiggo, take Davies. Wilko and I can hold the fort here. Stay on the air and don't do anything stupid."

"You ken me, Cap."

"Aye. That's what I'm worried about."

Wiggo climbed out of the manhole into a scene of chaos. Panicked people streamed out of the tube station entrance, screaming, some of them with torn clothing and bloodied noses or knees, all of them wide eyed in fear and shock at whatever had happened. The police were trying, mostly unsuccessfully, to herd them all in one direction, away from where the forensics team were trying to get the bodies from below organised. They may as well have been trying to herd cats.

Wiggo led Davies to the entranceway then tried to force his way against the flow into the crowd. It was hard going at first but when they reached the ticket hall the rush was already thinning out and by the time they got to the escalators they had the downward stairs to themselves.

Wiggo paused at the foot of the escalator to switch off his helmet light and told Davies to do the same.

"We might need them. Save the batteries now, avoid a fuckup later."

They found the source of the commotion in the westbound tunnel. A train was partially pulled into the station, only one carriage overlapping the platform. A uniformed tube employee, Wiggo guessed it to be the driver, stood by the train, gazing, mouth agape, at the vehicle. It was coated, floor to roof and nose to however far back they could see in the tunnel, with an oozing jelly-like substance that even now was flowing away, as if under its own volition, back into the darkness of the tunnel.

"What the fuck happened here, wee man?" Wiggo asked.

The driver shoved a cigarette in his mouth and took a deep drag before replying.

"It was right there, right in front of me. I couldn't stop. We went through it like a hot knife through butter, but it filled the tunnel for a long way and we were slowing and slowing and I thought we were going to get stuck so I sped up and we kept going and I couldn't see and then, blam, we were through to here. I opened the front door and all the passengers tumbled out like rats and then I was here on my own and now you're here and..."

It had all tumbled out of him in such a rush that he hadn't taken enough breath. His knees gave way beneath him and he would have fallen had Davies not held him up.

"He's in shock, Sarge," the private said. "We should get him up top."

"Hold him up for a sec," Wiggo said. "I need to check something out."

He left Davies with the driver and stepped, gingerly, forwards. Most of the gelatinous material had oozed away. He shone his rifle light down the tunnel. It reflected back from the train side where the now familiar oily, shimmering aurora hung in the dark air. His radio crackled in his ear, causing him to start.

"Wiggo? You there?"

"Aye, Cap."

"Meet me up top. The night shift is finished in Blackfriars and are coming over here to take over. We've been stood down until morning until they know what the fuck is going on."

"Aye? Well I wish them luck with that, for this is getting more peculiar by the minute."

Half an hour later they were back in their hotel. After a quick debrief in the bar over a round of whiskies, Wiggo took a double upstairs to his room and sipped at it while he picked up from where he'd left off in the notebook, at the door of the balloon shed   back   in   1956..

-THEN-

George and the other two lads returned a minute or two later, wheeling a wonky barrow that had been rather precariously stacked with jars of acid. I had them dump the whole bally lot down the drain in the shed before they caused another accident but I feared it was far too little, far too late.

I knew we needed to get down there after it, but before I could organize a proper hunt I had to spend minutes I could ill afford bringing the rest of the team up to date with the matter at hand.

"So exactly what is it?" Jennings, our administrator, accountant and all round worrier asked. He liked to be precise and clear on every matter but I had no answer that would satisfy him. Young George's reply was as good as any I could have managed.

"Clearly it's some kind of space poo," he said. "Shed-eating space poo. There, does naming it make it any better—any more understandable?"

After everyone had a laugh at Jennings' expense, I was able to start managing the situation. Jennings provided some answers to my many questions. The first, and most important, was as to the extent and nature of our sewage system—I'd never given it a moment's thought but our administrator seemed intimately familiar with it.

"We're on a main county line," he explained when I asked him. "Something my predecessor insisted on after the war when they were building the site. There's a new sewer right under our feet—an eight foot diameter brick channel that feeds directly into a main drain that goes through Anchester and down the valley before heading down toward Oxford for processing."

I could see the bally stuff in my mind's eye, slithering down there in the dark, heading for town and something to eat.

"Then we'd best get down there and stop this thing before it gets to that main drain," I said. I split the men up into four three-man teams, each with respirators and bottles of acid, and sent them down the valley to take up watching briefs in case our quarry got that far down the sewer.

Young George outdid himself by knocking up, in the five minutes it took me to find a flashlight, a small knapsack affair that, when squeezed under the arm like a bagpipe sac, fed acid down a metal tube to a pistol-grip nozzle that could be fired from my hand. I noted that he had even had time to make one for himself as he and I—with Jennings close behind—went down into the main drain under the shed, picking our way gingerly through the rubble.

The first thing I noted was the smell—even through the respirator mask the tang of the acid I'd had dumped down the hole was strong and acrid, threatening to burn at my nose and throat. We had descended right over the spot where the collapse had happened, but there was no sign of the ooze—although there was a distinct trail on the floor of the sewer to mark its passing that seemed to shine and shimmer in the beam from my flashlight. I motioned to the others that they should follow and I headed, at some speed, deeper into the tunnel.

At least the brickwork was new and hadn't crumbled—for a sewer, the tunnel was remarkably clean, and I came to almost be thankful for the stink of acid, for it surely masked many other stenches that might have proved rather more noxious. We were able to make good time—a fact that gave me some pause, for if we were making such rapid progress, then it meant that our quarry was moving just as quickly—and possibly even faster.

The first sign that it was still ahead of us came when my light fell on a partially digested rat. The head end still twitched and squealed in pain but from the ribs to where the tail should have been was just a mess of unregulated protoplasm, bubbling and seething—and growing. I had not considered that the ooze would be able to detach portions of goop and, in effect, multiply more rapidly—and now that I had thought of it, I could think of little else.

The poor beast beside my foot squealed piteously. I squirted acid on it and put it out of its misery with the heel of my boot—but even as I did so I heard more screams—all too human screams— coming up the tunnel from ahead of us.

I didn't wait for the other two—I ran, full pelt toward the hideous noises, the flashlight beam swinging wildly against the walls of the sewer ahead of me.

I was too late—far too late. The screaming stopped, leaving only the sound of my footsteps splashing in the puddles in the floor of the sewer and my breathing, loud and heavy inside the respirator. I rounded a long curve, then had to stop, all breath leaving me at the sight that awaited in the tunnel.

The ooze—protoplasm—whatever the hell it was, sat under an open manhole, pulled up into a dome almost six feet in diameter, the bulk of it almost filling the tunnel. One of the crews I'd sent to keep watch were embedded inside it, partially melted, skin and bone and clothes in the process of being assimilated into the matrix, three grown men, all already, thankfully, dead as the flesh sloughed from their bones.

I heard young George bring up his lunch in the tunnel behind me. Someone else—Jennings probably, began to weep quietly but I forced myself to step closer. I raised the pistol grip, squeezed the bag under my arm, and sprayed the ooze with acid.

The result was immediate—it recoiled, as if struck, a wobble travelling all the way through it. As I had seen before in the laboratory it pulled itself into a tighter ball then started to half-slump, half-roll away down the tunnel. The result of that retreat was that the three partially eaten bodies of my friends were unceremoniously deposited in the sewer at my feet, but I had no time for grief—the ooze was already retreating away from me at some speed.

I stepped over the bodies and headed after it but as fast as I could spray acid it could retreat faster. I had at least succeeded in slowing its growth—it was half the size it had been as it disappeared at an alarming haste into the darkness beyond the reach of my light.

Even then I might have followed had I not heard a cry from behind me. I turned to see Jennings shouting up to someone up above the open drain cover. I was torn between pressing my small advantage and my curiosity. Curiosity—and common sense—won in the end, and I returned back up the tunnel to stand under the manhole.

Jennings was talking animatedly to one of the other search crews I'd sent out. I left him to it and went to young George's aid. Despite his obvious distaste and nausea, he was intent on checking the three bodies—obviously intent on trying to save them—but it was clear to me that the men were far gone.

"It's all my fault," the lad was saying, over and over again, trying for a pulse on an arm that was barely attached to the molten remains of what had been a shoulder and rib cage. I had to bodily drag him away and had Jennings tend to him while I caught up with the men above. In truth, there wasn't much to hear—although what there was chilled me to the bone. This was the last manhole before town—and the slime was now surely on its way there.

I almost felt the blood drain from my face. Anchester wasn't big, but it had a population of almost ten thousand. I looked at the bodies at my feet and tried to picture that scene, multiplied a hundred fold and more. Seconds later I was running, full pelt, down the tunnel. I was vaguely aware of George and Jennings behind me, also running, calling my name, but I had no thought for them.

George had been wrong on one thing—it wasn't his fault. They were my men—my responsibility. Any fault was mine and mine alone.

And I was not about to let any more people die due to my negligence.

I came to a junction some five minutes after leaving the open manhole. The new red brick tunnel gave way to a much older sewer—dank and wet, dripping with thick slimy moss and lichen, and ankle deep in black water. Now that I no longer had the tang of acid to keep the smell at bay I noticed the stench, thick, almost chewable. Only the respirator mask prevented me from having to stop and even then I was almost choking as I headed left—downhill—toward Anchester.

I did not have to go far before I once again heard screams—from above me now, in the streets of the town. George and Jennings caught up with me as I was trying to heave a manhole cover aside to give me access up to the road above. Between the three of us we managed to push the heavy circle of iron up and out of the way. If I was worried that we might disrupt traffic I needn't have bothered— traffic was more than adequately disturbed already.

I climbed up out of the sewer into a scene of utter chaos.

The first thing I saw was an overturned butcher's van—it had been in collision with a horse and cart in the middle of the main street. Two older ladies tended to the butcher—he was bleeding profusely from a head wound and was clearly in a daze. His livelihood, the meat from his van, was strewn all across the road, as was the contents of the cart—old iron, clothing scraps and books by the look of it. The cart driver had got the worst of things—his body lay, already mostly eaten, in the center of a mass of oozing protoplasm. The poor horse lay beside its master. The bulk of it was partially digested. Thankfully the ooze had caught it at the front end first so its death would have been quick at least. But the back legs were still kicking, even as flesh sloughed off its back. I looked away, back to the ooze. The horse's head was already little more than sludge and goop; lumps of tissue and blood were visible in the clear protoplasm, clearly being drawn to a spot in the interior of the oozing mass.

The screaming was coming from two children, too frightened to run, too amazed at the sight in the street to take their eyes off it. By rights I should have done something to comfort them, but the digestive processes of the ooze had caught my gaze. As I said, it was clearly taking its sustenance down toward a central part of its bulk—and if that was the case, I knew that there must be some sense to its structure, some degree of organization.

And something with organization could become disorganized, in the right circumstances.

I watched the poor horse be digested as first George, then Jennings pulled themselves up out of the sewer to stand beside me.

"We need to focus our attack," I said as George raised his pistol to point it at the ooze. "And we need to coordinate it too. Follow my lead."

The ooze was growing visibly, throbbing and

swelling as it assimilated the bulk of the horse and the meat from the van. A crowd had gathered in the street, keeping a discreet distance, the townspeople clearly unsure what to make of this new thing in their midst. Some of the more curious of them were already encroaching perilously close to the protoplasm and if I did not take charge of matters soon, someone else was going to get hurt—or killed.

"With me, George," I said, and stepped forward. I ignored the closest parts of the ooze and aimed my pistol at the central portion, aiming at the spot where most of the digested matter seemed to be being transported. Blood and pink tissue flowed inward, a grotesque mockery of a circulatory system. I aimed for the central area and squeezed the trigger. George sent a stream of acid at almost exactly the same spot.

I hoped we would be able to end it there and then as the plasm bubbled and hissed, but I had forgotten how speedy the dashed thing could be. It immediately recoiled away from the acid and from us, heading off down the cobbled street, scattering the watching crowd in front of it, leaving a trail of bloody slime in its wake. I hosed the slimy remains down with acid, remembering the rat, and how there was life in the ooze, even in the remnants it left behind, then turned my attention to the rapidly departing protoplasm.

"After it, George, quickly," I called. "We can't let it get away." The pair of us, with Jennings close behind, ran in pursuit, leaving the startled townspeople far behind as the chase took us the length of the High Street.

We got close enough on two occasions to send more acid over the bulk of it, but the central portion—the place where a ball of partially digested bloody matter still hung—continued to elude us—and the ooze was capable of moving faster than we could run.

We pursued it through the town, squirting acid at any globs of material it left in its wake, before finally catching up to it on the riverbank near the Rowing Club. It slithered quickly down the jetty and spread out, like a huge cape, across almost the full width of the river. An oily, shimmering glow seemed to rise from the water, even as I squeezed the trigger, over and over again, until the pack was completely empty of acid.

The current flowed past us, and the ooze sank, slowly, out of sight. I raised my gaze from the water and looked downstream.

The city of Oxford lay directly ahead—and the ooze was being taken right to it.

"We're going to need bigger knapsacks," George said.

-WIGGO-

Wiggo was eager to turn the page to know what came next but was interrupted by a pounding on his door.

"No rest for the wicked," the captain said when Wiggo answered and opened the door. "We're going back in. They've lost the night shift lads."

The next five minutes were frantic as they headed for the truck and got kitted out again, but as they headed back into the center Wiggo found some quiet time and could not resist going back to the notebook; he wasn't far from the end now, and wanted to reach the conclusion.

-THEN-

I was kept busy for the rest of that long day—arranging for everywhere, and everything, the ooze might have touched to be washed down with acid and—a much harder task in the end—attempting to impress on the authorities the seriousness of the situation facing us. It didn't help my case that the thing seemed to have gone to ground so to speak—all that afternoon I had teams out looking for signs of it up and down the riverbanks, but to no avail. As evidence, I had a butcher with a sore head and a whole lot of bloody, acid-scarred, slime—certainly not enough to convince the Ministry to give me any special attention, despite the fact that some of it was the remains of dead members of my team.

"We've got a bally flap on in Gibraltar," the clipped tones on the other end of the phone said. "We don't have the time or the manpower to waste on any blasted jelly from outer space. Please don't be bothering us again unless you've got something that needs our urgent attention. You're a rocket group, aren't you? Well just blow the bloody thing up and have an end to it."

Tempting as the idea might be, launching a rocket on the academia in Oxford wasn't really an option. I could only keep a watching brief, prepare as well as I could for any eventuality, and hope that I could control any resultant mayhem without any further loss of life.

At least I had the local constabulary on my side, for two officers had seen what happened on Anchester High Street. One of them, Sergeant Green, was a seasoned veteran and level headed enough that his superiors couldn't ignore his story. By the time night fell I had a team of firemen, the Oxford police force and my own staff at my disposal. George and Jennings had arranged, by hook or by crook, for a delivery of industrial acid to be shipped to us. Instead of water, the firemen had access to a tanker of acid and a generator to pressurize it in their hoses—the hoses themselves might not survive for long—but I was hoping that they wouldn't have to.

I sat in the main police station in Oxford, smoked too many cigarettes and drank far too much strong, sweet tea. I racked my brains, knowing that I must have missed something in my preparations, at the same time feeling ever increasing guilt creep up on me over the death of my friends and companions.

When the inevitable call finally came and we had to move, I was actually glad of the action.

It must have been in the sewers—two manholes, both melted and fused as if eaten away, lay on the cobbles, discarded as it oozed, like toothpaste from a too-strongly squeezed tube, up out of the drains, its bulk slowly filling the parking crescent in front of the railway station. Wherever it had been, it had obviously been feeding—it kept coming, and coming, until it lay in a heap almost six feet tall across an area the size of a soccer penalty box. The clear matrix was shot through with red veins, its transport system for taking food back to the central mass. And as I got closer I saw what it had been feeding on; half a dozen cows and several sheep—or what was left of them—hung suspended in the ooze, none of them much more than bags of skin and semi-digested bone. The whole mass of the plasm shimmered in the moonlight, and again I saw the same colors I had seen under the scope—greens and blues and gold hanging in the air above it like a curtain of fine gauze.

The railway's stationmaster had been the one to call us and he was clearly flustered, in a situation he did not know how to control or apply to a timetable. He was addressing Sergeant Green, his voice raised almost in a shout.

"What in blazes are you going to do about this then? I can't have this mess on the concourse—the 8:10 from Reading will be coming in any minute now—then what am I going to do?"

The sergeant had the small man taken back into the station but we could all still hear him, promising that he'd be having 'a word with our superiors.'

"Good luck with that," I muttered, with what would be the last bit of levity for a while as the ooze started to creep—not toward the station but toward the main road.

We only just got the fire crew in position in time as the ooze advanced, crawling over a parked car and stripping its paint job as if it was sandpaper. Sergeant Green gave the order and two hoses started to send an arc of acid over the top of the protoplasm—I had already told them to seek out the central digestive mass. The ooze bubbled and hissed—and once again I thought we had it beat, only to be proved wrong.

It surged—I have no other word to describe it—and moved in one smooth motion. We thought we had it contained between the railway station and the tall wall on the other side of the road but the thing flowed up and away and over before we'd scarcely begun to hose it down.

By the time we got round the other side of the wall there was nothing to be seen but a long trail of what looked like partially burned grass across a once-perfect lawn, and some slime draped over the walls and roof of one of the college buildings. It made the old stone shimmer and radiate as if coated in hot oil and in other circumstances might even have been quite beautiful.

So began a long night where we played a dangerous game of hide and seek. The ooze showed up twice more—each time larger than the last, each time arising out of the sewer system, and each time retreating so fast from our acid attack that we were unable to stop it. As dawn approached, I realized that the town would be waking up, and with it the chance of many more casualties. I could see no other course of action but to take the fight to where the thing was most comfortable—I was going to have to go down into the main sewer.

The firemen, stout chaps that they were, offered to go down in my place but I felt the burden of responsibility heavy on my shoulders. I had them show me how to operate the nozzles of their hoses. As I was suiting up into one of their safety suits young George started to do the same beside me.

"It's my fault too, Prof," he said as I made to stop him. "I'm coming, and that's that. If you want to put a note in my jotter later, so be it. But I'm coming."

In truth I was glad of the company as we went gingerly down one of the main manholes into the sewer under the railway station—the first place we had encountered it earlier in the evening. The two hoses were lowered down to us and we stood there for several minutes as our eyes accustomed to the gloom. I heard the thrum of the generator overhead—the acid was ready and waiting for when we needed it. I only hoped it would be enough.

"Well, here we are then," George said. "What's the plan, Prof?"

"Keep talking—make some noise," I replied, thinking on my feet. "I think it's attracted by sound—our men in the sewer, the butcher's van, the railway station itself—all noise."

"You mean, we're the bait?"

I laughed—the sound echoed around us in the confines of the sewer.

"If you want to put it that way, yes."

"In that case, I've got just the thing."

George then surprised me by starting to sing, loudly and making up in effort what he lacked in musicality.

"I am the Lord High Executioner, a personage of noble rank and title."

It delighted me so much, there in that dark place, that I joined in with all the gusto I could manage.

We had got as far as the second 'I've got a little list' when the light in the tunnel changed—

somewhere to our north something shimmered, greens and blues and gold—and it was getting closer. George noticed it and almost faltered in his singing, but I took up the slack, and belted out another chorus as the protoplasm oozed into view, the bulk of it completely filling the sewer as it came forward, heading straight for us.

George looked over at me and even in the gloom I saw that his eyes had gone wide with fear, but he stood beside me as I hefted the heavy hose at my waist, and he followed suit.

We stopped singing as the tunnel filled with a dancing aurora of color that hissed and buzzed as if in response to our song.

"Ready?" I said.

George nodded, and I twisted the nozzle.

As before the result was immediate. The protoplasm leapt away from us, retreating back in the tunnel. And even as I stepped forward to follow, I realized I had indeed forgotten something—the tang of acid and seared protoplasm threatened to choke me... and I wasn't wearing a respirator mask.

But the ooze was getting away again, and this might be my last chance to prevent early morning chaos in the city above. I walked forward fast, spraying ahead of me, my rubber boots splashing in acid, slime and bubbling, popping pustules of protoplasm. George came along at my side as we chased the thing along the sewer.

I had to hold my breath as I went as the fumes got too noxious, and I was more than aware that we would run out of length of hose any second—but we were, finally, winning. The ooze stopped retreating and formed into a ball some four feet across, a ball that got smaller and smaller as we washed it in acid, sloughing its surface off, revealing the partially digested material at the center.

I was almost out of breath, and the hose was at its maximum length, but I had enough of both remaining to step forward. I thrust the hose—and my hands along with it-deep in the center of the remaining ooze, and let the acid blow it apart into bubbling drips of slime that gave out one last dancing aurora of color then, finally, fell quiet and dark.

They say my burns will heal, although I will always have scars on my hands and feet to forever remind me of the thing that came from the sky. But it is not as if I need much reminding. George is here in the bed beside me in the sanitarium—we are allowed out into the garden for a smoke before bed last thing in the evening, and last night it was a clear, moonless night. We looked up, and there, high above us, the sky was dancing and humming, in greens and blues and gold.

Someday soon, we will go and meet it again.

And this time we will be better prepared for the encounter.

-WIGGO-

The truck came to a halt just as Wiggo finished. He waved the notebook at Captain Banks.

"Cap? We need to talk about this."

"It'll have to wait. We've got men in harm's way down there somewhere. They come first."

Wiggo nodded and shoved the notebook back inside his jacket before following the captain out.

They were back at the High Holborn to New Oxford Street intersection. It was now somewhere on the other side of midnight. The forensic lads had taken the remains away to their lab for testing, the crowds had dispersed, the traffic was light and a strange quiet lay over the scene. The captain had them take their rifles and handguns. They each had a hard hat with a headlight and radio as their contribution to the health and safety rules. The younger of the two workmen was standing over the open manhole waiting for them.

Wiggo laughed.

"You look like you'd rather be anywhere else but here, lad," he said.

"You're right," came the reply. "But if I don't do it, who will?"

Wiggo clapped him on the shoulder

"We'll make a sodjer of you yet, son. Lead on."

He followed the workman back down into the sewer. The forensics team had left the lights on, which allowed the squad to make quick passage through to the chamber where the bodies had been found. They all stopped and looked down into the strangely smooth-walled tunnel that descended into blackness.

"I was listening on the radio," the workman said, and went even whiter than previously. "They went down there, then there was gunfire and shouting and then screaming then...nothing."

"How long ago was this?" Banks asked.

"Nearly an hour now. If they were coming back out, they'd be here by now, surely?"

"Not necessarily," Wiggo replied. "And don't call me Shirley."

That at least got him a thin smile in reply. When they went down into the tunnel Wiggo went first.

It wasn't so steep they were in danger of tumbling headlong into the dark, but it was steep enough that care was needed and Wiggo took it slowly, sweeping the area ahead with both headlight and gun light before descending, half a dozen paces at a time. Shadows danced and flickered from the others' lights and more than once Wiggo jerked, and almost fired when he confused some of the shifting darkness for movement ahead. The going underfoot was soft, almost rubbery, and after a time Wiggo began to notice definite footprints embedded there; heavy duty boots. Soldiers' boots.

They went down for ten minutes.

"Where does this go?" Wiggo asked the workman.

"Buggered if I know," the lad replied. "It wasn't even here three days ago when we came through the sewer up above."

"No, I mean generally," Wiggo said. "Are there tube tunnels below here?"

"Probably. There's all kinds of shit down here. Wartime bunkers, old mail railway tracks, ancient sewers long since disused, even Roman temples. But as for the tube, yes, the central line's down here somewhere."

Wiggo was thinking of the glistening, dripping train they'd found in the station and of how deep the escalators had been. If his mental calculations were right, they should be nearly at that level now. He was proved right a minute later when the tunnel opened out, not into the tube system, but into what appeared to be one of the old disused sewers.

Pale lichens hung from the crumbling brick of the walls. There had been minor collapses in places, small piles of tumbled brick and dirt lying at irregular intervals. In other places the walls were smeared with the ever more familiar glistening slime, as if they had been brushed by something in its passing through. Wiggo found another two clear army-issue boot-prints in one of the fallen patches of dirt. They looked fresher. Wiggo upped his pace, unsure whether he was following the soldiers' footprints or the trail of slime. He was worried that it wouldn't matter which.

Two minutes after that they found the soldiers.

There was little to nothing left of them save bones and weaponry, all else having been dissolved down and gone to feed the hunger of their attacker. Having read the journal, Wiggo now had a clear

image in his head of what it must be. It didn't make
the sight of the dead any easier to behold. The
young workman took himself off to one side and
was violently sick. Captain Banks tried to reach
someone up top on his radio, then had Wiggo try
when there was no answer. Wiggo got only
crackling static on his attempt.

"We're going to get forensics down here," Banks
said.

"We're going to get the fuck out of here, that's
what we're going to do," the workman said and
without waiting turned back to head for the tunnel
upward. Something slithered moistly in the sewer
and when Wiggo turned his gaze that way he saw
that the passageway was blocked completely by a
glistening tube of what could only be described as
tightly packed slime.

The workman appeared to be rooted to the spot,
unable to take his gaze off the thing that was oozing
towards him. It was almost translucent and Wiggo
saw things floating in what passed for its digestive
system: chunks of red meat that didn't bear thinking
about. It was getting ever closer to the young
workman.

"Get back here, you fucking idiot," Wiggo
shouted. The lad didn't move. A slender pseudopod
slid out, sinuous and snake-like, making for the
workman's feet. Wiggo stepped quickly forward and
put two rounds into the tissue. It splattered on the
ground like a burst balloon, and immediately ran
and flowed like oil on a hot skillet, reforming itself
almost as fast as it had been blown apart.

The rest of the squad came up beside Wiggo and

put several volleys into the body of the amorphous blob, all with the same result; pieces of it were blown off and scattered but within seconds they had flowed back to be reconstituted back into the main mass. The only other result was to apparently anger the thing. It surged in the tunnel and came forward fast, a wave of protoplasm that washed over the workman's feet, knees and hips, up to his chest before he had time to scream. He put out a hand. Wiggo had to drop his rifle to take it, and that split-second was enough to seal the man's fate. Wiggo's fingertips barely touched the outstretched hand then the man was pulled, sucked, away, protoplasm filling his mouth and silencing his screams forever. Even as Wiggo took up his gun again the blob was pulling away back down the tunnel, the body of the workman clearly to be seen, still struggling weakly, engulfed totally inside.

Wiggo moved to give chase but Banks stopped him with a barked order.

"No. Not with these weapons," he said. "We need to get forensics down here, but before that, we're going to need the right tool for the job. It's time you told me what's in that journal. And it's time we got this analysed."

Wiggo turned to see that the captain had scooped up some of the protoplasm into his hard hat. The hard plastic was notched, almost melted in places, but seemed to be holding the material in the bottom of the bowl, material which seethed and roiled, as if desperate for escape. Wiggo saw that the captain held it out away from his body and took great care not to spill any as they headed back up to the relative   sanity   of   the   London   streets.

-WIGGO -

Back up top, Wiggo and the two privates stood off at one side having a smoke while the captain firstly handed off his 'sample' to the forensics team then got on the radio. Wiggo saw Banks having an animated, nearly angry, conversation and guessed the flame-throwers weren't on the verge of turning up any time soon. He was replaying the death of the workman in his mind, over and over, wondering if he'd reacted quickly enough, wondering if the man could have been saved. He was almost thankful to be disturbed by a cough at his back. He turned and saw the old man standing at the crowd barrier.

"George Thornton, I presume?" Wiggo said.

"You read it then?"

"Every word. I have questions."

"I'm sure you do. I was thinking we could chat over breakfast. Do you fancy a pint?"

Wiggo introduced George to the rest of the squad. The captain joined them.

"We've got a couple of hours until the kit we need gets here. Nobody's going back down there until I give the say so," Banks said.

"Good," Wiggo replied. "For the old lad here has the best idea I've heard all night."

Five minutes later they were sitting around a table in The Kingsway Tavern. George obviously had some clout with someone; the bar had been opened just for them and the owner fetched and carried beer and cheese and onion toasties, almost obsequious in his deference to the old man.

"Benefits of a lifetime in some of the murkier parts of the Civil Service," George explained. "A man learns some useful tricks of the trade."

"I'd like to learn this one," Wiggo said, then sat back to enjoy his beer while George retold the story Wiggo had read in the journal. There was more of George in it this time, rather than the almost dry telling of the Prof and the old man proved to be a consummate storyteller, peppering the tale with anecdotes about the people involved and providing enough local color that Wiggo could almost see it unfold in his mind. He was surprised to find their third pint arriving just as George was bringing the story to an end.

He peeled off an ancient pair of cracked leather clothes and showed the squad his hands, poor, ravaged things, the extent of the damage still apparent more than sixty years on.

"I got this helping the Prof out of the sewer system in Oxford. Just don't get any on you," he said. "The Prof got it even worse than me; he lived in pain for the rest of his years. Passed in '96, poor chap, but was never really the same again. We kept watch together, he and I, until age caught up with him. And it's caught up with me too. Now it's here and I'm too buggering old to do much about it. But if you chaps believe me, then I can finally pass on the baton."

"We believe you," Wiggo said. "Are fire and acid

the only things that work against it?"

"Well, we didn't have time to try any exotic biologicals on it," George replied. "But yes, the acid in particular worked just fine. But we needed a lot of it. Any idea how big it's got? I get the impression it must be pretty large."

"Aye, you could say that," Wiggo replied and turned to Banks. "How many tankers did you order, Cap?"

"Enough, I hope," the captain replied with a worried frown.

They turned down a fourth pint. Old George seemed disappointed.

"We'll catch up when this is all over," Wiggo promised him. "Then we'll both have a barrel of ale and swap stories. You're no' the only one with tall tales to tell, auld yin. Get yourself home and have a kip. You've earned it."

"Home's not the same since the wife passed," the old man said sadly. "No, I'll be here. I'll be around. Having been there at the beginning, I need to see how this ends."

That was a feeling Wiggo knew only too well. He shook hands, carefully, with George and they left him starting on another pint and another toastie while the barman bowed and scraped.

"That's definitely a trick I need to learn," Wiggo muttered to himself as they went back out to the High Holborn junction. Dim daylight was trying to make itself known through low clouds. People had gathered to gawk at the barriers again and the annoyed honking of stuck traffic rose from all the surrounding streets. Captain Banks went in search of news about their requested kit. Wiggo took the privates aside for a smoke, fighting off an urge to head back to the bar and keep the auld lad company. It was just as well he did for the captain returned a minute later, and this time he was smiling.

"The tankers are on their way, and the flame-throwers are already here. Look lively, lads. It's payback time."

-WIGGO-

They had a five minute demo of the operation of the compact flame-thrower packs from a curt, serious-minded officer who had been charged with their delivery.

"I thought these were banned?" Davies said as he adjusted the straps of his weapon.

"They are, lad," Banks replied. "The Lord knows where they dug this lot up from. They're M2A1-7s, Yank issue and at least forty years old. Some quartermaster's been sitting on them in a storeroom while they gathered dust. But they've all been tested. They'll work just fine as long as we don't point them at each other. Remember though, short, controlled bursts. We'll only get ten seconds tops out of each one."

"Backup?" Wiggo asked, and Banks shook his head.

"We're it, at least until the tankers turn up. They're coming from a factory in Oxfordshire and should be here sometime later this morning. My plan is to track this fucker down to wherever it hides and, if we can't kill it, we can at least contain it until we can get the acid on it."

Wiggo was remembering the size of the thing in the tunnel, and calculating the odds. Forty seconds of flame between them certainly going to do some damage. Whether it was going to be enough remained to be seen. He shook his tanks. Something sloshed sluggishly inside.

"So it's kerosene, is it?" he said.

The dour officer who'd given them the demo replied.

"No. It's a gel produced by mixing fuel with M4 thickening compound. Same load, but greater range."

"How far are we talking?"

"Up to fifty meters," came the reply. "But from what I can gather from your captain here, you're expecting close up work. You'll need to be careful. Any backwash could take you out with it."

"Just what I needed. Something else to worry about." Wiggo strapped on the pack and turned to Davies and Wilkins. "And remember, no sudden farting. Wouldn't want to get caught in any backwash."

Wiggo had the backpack on over the top of his flak vest. He carried the flame-thrower, his handgun, three clips for the pistol and four stun grenades. He put on the hard helmet with the headlight which would be their only lighting in the deeper areas. The radio immediately crackled in his ear. It was forensics with a report for the captain on the sample they'd recovered. It didn't tell them anything they didn't already know. It was a biological, protoplasmic material, origin unknown.

"A fucking alien in other words," Wiggo muttered. "Same as it ever was."

With all the gear on, going down the manhole was a bit of a tight squeeze but once in the sewer they had plenty of room, although Wiggo was all too aware he was carrying four stone or so of extra weight. It was like a training exercise, although at least here they didn't have mountains to climb or snow to contend with.

The captain was in the lead as they reached the smooth walled tunnel and left the last of the lighting behind, heading downward. Davies and Wilkins were right behind him. Wiggo waited until the small team of six forensics folk went past then tagged along at the rear. He kept an eye on their back during the descent; the beastie had crept up on them once before and he wasn't about to let that happen again.

The captain took it slow and careful but they reached the bottom tunnel with no problems. Wiggo saw that the walls glistened, rainbow aurora reflecting back at them. The thing wasn't here at the moment, but it had been, not too long ago. He kept a tighter grip on the pistol grip of the flame-thrower as they headed for the spot where they'd found the bodies.

The next few hours passed painfully slowly. The forensics folk did their slow, careful work on the remains while the squad patrolled the boundaries of the scene. Nothing of much interest happened, although Wiggo was glad of the fact that there was no sign of the poor workman's body anywhere in the tunnel. It was only as the forensics team were carrying the remains away that the action picked up.

A scream, distant but definitely human, rose up from somewhere deeper in the tunnel system. Captain Banks was immediately on the move, as if he'd been expecting it.

"Right," he said to the forensics team. "You lot leg it back up top, fast as you like. We'll give you a minute to get safe and watch your backs. Then it's show   time."

-WIGGO-

The minute seemed to last for five. The forensics team was gone and away back up the tunnel and there was no sound of any commotion from that direction. The captain waited a few more seconds then led the squad out, heading at double time down deeper in the tunnel in the direction of the scream.

Another wail came up from below, closer now. Wiggo was forced to break into a run to keep up with the captain, feeling the weight of the tank drag against his shoulders with every step. More screams rent the air; they were running directly towards them now, but quickly found their way blocked by a rusty iron door that looked like it hadn't been opened in decades. The wails of terror were coming from the other side of it.

"Get some weight on that, lads," Banks said. "See if you can get it open."

Wilkins tried first but succeeded only in forcing the old metal to emit some creaks and groans.

"Here, let a man at it," Davies said and pushed his way forward. The private strained and groaned and succeeded in forcing it open an inch. That let Wiggo step up beside him and get his fingers around the edge of the door enough to help drag it open. It swung towards them with a fingernail-on-blackboard shriek of metal on stone that was answered by more cries of terror from the other side. Wiggo was first out the door, and stepped out onto a thin walkway looking over the Aldwych tube station. The station itself looked to have been disused for some years but there was a train stopped on the far side of the tracks from where Wiggo stood and the screams were coming from there. He couldn't see what was going on; the train itself was blocking his view. But it sounded like bloody murder.

The rest of the squad came through at his back and Banks pushed past.

"Quick as you like, lads. Sounds like we're needed over there. Don't touch the rails though; we want to make yon thing crispy, not us."

Wiggo followed gingerly. They made their way round the back end of the train and pulled themselves up onto the platform opposite. They looked along the length of the carriages at a scene from hell.

The front end of the train was completely embedded in a mass of protoplasmic blob which pulsated in waves as it pushed itself out of the tunnel at the far end of the station and crept over the front carriages and along the platform. A mass of people were trying to flee, piled up in a thrashing, screaming, bloody mob against the small opening that appeared to be the only way off the platform. The blob was just feet away from them, and what looked like a score of people fought and bit and tramped in their frenzy to escape.

The blob surged, washing in a wave over the half a dozen people nearest to it. High screams echoed around the old station. The captain was already on the move, running towards the entrance. Wiggo followed, with the two privates close on his heels. He felt for the trigger on the wand in his hand, but as they closed on the mayhem, he realized the flame-throwers could not be used; there were already eight people trapped in the matrix of the blob. If they torched the thing, they'd be killing civilians at the same time. Banks had obviously had the same thought. They arrived at the scene just as the bottleneck broke and the escapees forced their way through to a stairwell beyond. Their screams diminished into the distance as they climbed. The squad were left with the sight of the blob slowly oozing over the eight people it had trapped. Three of them were already totally engulfed, although not yet dead, struggling feebly, mouths gasping for breath while the foul stuff forced its way down their throats. Davies, his medical instincts kicking in, moved forward, intent on reaching into the matrix to get at the people.

"No, stand back," Banks barked. "That's an order, Private. We don't touch this stuff. It'll have you in there along with them in no time."

"Then what do we do, Cap?" Wiggo said. "I'm not sure I can just stand here and watch these people die."

Four more civilians stood, waist deep in the matrix, clawing at it with their hands, struggling to fight against it but obviously held solidly in place. All four howled in miserable agony. Wiggo saw the captain look further along the platform.

"You're right, Wiggo," Banks said. "We have to try something. Let's see if we can cut this end off from the main mass. If it's got some kind of central brain somewhere, maybe if we disconnect it…"

Wiggo caught the captain's gist immediately and moved with him, skirting between the train and the blob and sidling along the platform towards where the bulk of the thing was still oozing out of the tunnel. Banks picked a spot some ten feet from the trapped civilians and pointed.

"Concentrate the fire there. Two seconds each should be enough to tell us if it'll work."

Wiggo pulled the trigger. Fire flew with a whoosh of warmth that surprised him with its intensity, the wand washing flame over a five yard wide patch of the thing. The result was immediate; the bulk of the blob drew back into the tunnel as if hit by a lightning bolt. Wiggo released the trigger and went to leap after the departing thing but Banks pulled him back.

"No, look."

The second effect of the flames had been to disincorporate the other part of the blob from its matrix. It sloughed off the civilians like water, running to the ground and pouring in the same quicksilver manner they'd seen before, back along the platform in the direction of the tunnel. Wiggo had to dance back to avoid some that appeared to be intent on flowing over his boots.

"Let me torch it, Cap," Wiggo said.

"No. Save it. We might need it. We need to get these civilians seen to."

The four people who had been totally embedded in the matrix were most definitely dead, which

Wiggo thought was a blessing in disguise given the state of those left alive. All of their clothing...and most of their skin...below the waist was fused together, as if quickly melted then just as quickly hardened. All four were still screaming, lost in a world of pain. Davies used up most of the morphine in his field medical kit just to get them calmed.

"Can they be moved?" Banks asked. "We need to get up top and find out what the fuck is going on."

"I doubt if anybody kens any more than we do," Wiggo muttered under his breath, then moved quickly to help Davies who had decided it would be better to move the people than to leave them on the platform. Captain Banks, meanwhile, was trying to reach someone on his radio headset. Wiggo was party to the conversation, but heard only hissing static in reply to the captain's call.

"Looks like we're on our own, lads," Banks said.

"Same as it ever was," Wiggo answered, and got a grim smile in reply.

Each of the squad took one person each. It was like handling a dead weight. Wiggo's new companion was a middle-aged woman, smartly dressed, at least what was left of it, maybe even a looker on her day. Now she was little more than a ball of pain and hurt and judging by her wounds that was going to be the extent of her life for a while. Wiggo got her as far as the staircase then looked up, and up. There were at least a dozen flights to climb, while carrying the dead weight of the woman, and the extra weight of the flame-thrower.

"I suppose a lift is out of the question?"

Banks pointed to their left. There was a lift shaft

there, but it bore a graffiti-covered Out of Order sign that looked like it had been there for at least a decade. Wiggo put the flame-thrower wand in the holster at the side of the canister, lifted the woman in both hands with her head lolling on his right shoulder and started up the stairwell. He knew after half a dozen steps that this was going to take a while.

-WIGGO-

Wiggo heard the others' heavy footsteps on the stairs behind him. The woman he carried had, thankfully, lapsed into unconsciousness, free from pain for the moment at least. Wiggo looked up the stairwell. There was brighter light up there, still a long way away and she was already feeling too heavy in his arms. He called out.

"Need some help down here."

There was no reply save his own voice echoing back at him. His calf muscles joined his arms in complaining. He kept climbing, managed three more flights, then had to stop on a landing to catch his breath and let some of the lactic acid build up clear away. The others climbed up to join him, each of them clearly as out of breath as he was.

All four of the wounded were out cold when they were gently laid down, sitting with their backs to the inner stairwell railings.

"That's some bloody good gear you've got in yon wee kit of yours," Wiggo said to Davies. "I don't suppose you've got anything that'll help wi' this fucking climbing?"

'I've got some fags, Sarge?" Davies said, laughing.

"Hand one over then, lad. I'm already gasping."

Davies passed round the cigarettes and they smoked in silence.

"It's too quiet, Cap," Wiggo said after a minute

or so. "Given that lot that rushed out of here, surely somebody should have come to investigate by now? A copper, if nobody else?"

"I've been thinking the same thing. I don't like it."

"That makes two of us."

There had still been no sound from above by the time they finished their smokes. When Wiggo bent to lift the woman, he got a clear view down the whole depth of the stairwell and was relieved to be able to see the light leaking in from the platform at the bottom; he had half expected to see the stairs had been flooded with a wash of the protoplasm. It was a thought he immediately regretted as he started to climb again, for now, in his mind's eye, he could see the blob filling the stairwell below them, creeping up ever closer at their backs.

He concentrated on the climb.

As they neared the top, he heard sound seeping down from above, but it was not reassuring. It sounded like more screaming.

A lot more screaming.

After what seemed like an age, he reached the top and carried the woman across the floor of a derelict ticket hall. The noise was all coming from beyond that, out in the street. There was no mistaking it, it was definitely screams, mingled with the crash and crump of vehicle collisions, the blaring of car horns and a distant wail of sirens.

The rest of the squad joined him in sitting the unconscious injured down in a row of seats lined along the inner wall of the station before heading to the doorway. There had been a barricaded door in the not too distant past. Its bloodied remains lay on the pavement, testament to the fleeing people who had barrelled through it. They had been fleeing the horrors of the tube station, only to run out into even more mayhem and terror.

Wiggo and the squad stood at the top of a short flight of six steps down to the street level, or rather, where street level had been. The road was knee deep in the protoplasmic material for as far as they could see in either direction. Cars, buses, taxis and people were all stuck in it. The lucky ones were still protected inside their vehicles. The unlucky ones were already being assimilated, still screaming, into the matrix. Some had climbed up onto car roofs but there was no escape there; the blob seethed and surged as if aware of its prey's hiding places, swamping the cars with waves of material to get to the people on top.

Wiggo had seen plenty of disaster movies set in London, but somehow the reality was more immediate, and much the worse for it. Captain Banks was the first to shake off the shock of the sight.

"Buckle up, lads," he said. "Let's see if we can get some of this shite cleared away."

"What about the wounded?" Davies asked.

Wiggo waved at the carnage in front of them as he unholstered the wand.

"I think they're safer where they are for the time being, don't you?"

When the captain stepped forward, Wiggo was right at his side, finger on the trigger.

They both fired at the same time, a two second burst aimed at the foot of the steps and an area where there were no cars or pedestrians. As before, the effect was immediate; the blob retreated as if hit by an electric shock. It began to pile up deeper on the far side of the road, trying to escape down an alleyway to the side of the Savoy Hotel. Banks turned to Wiggo.

"Take Wilkins, see how much you can get of it. Davies and I will clear this part and look after the injured. Whatever happens, be back here in five. Don't make me come and get you."

Wiggo motioned Wilkins forward.

"You've got five shots, I've got three. Let's see if we can torch this fucker."

The blob had retreated fast, leaving the road clear. Dead and dying lay strewn on the ground and the road was blocked by vehicles desperately trying to restart engines that had seconds before been clogged. The sound of sirens seemed closer; the rescue teams were incoming. Wiggo had no time to wait for them. The blob had piled itself into the alleyway, where it had the space filled to a height of eight feet or more.

"Torch it," Wiggo shouted. "Burn the buggering thing."

Wilkins sent out a jet of flame that shot across the intervening space in an arc and fell full across the bulk of the blob. Even as it burned it was retreating farther back in the alley, sloughing off blackened pieces of itself as it went. Wilkins still had his finger on the trigger, three, four seconds' worth of flame washing over the thing.

Wiggo pulled the private's hand off the wand.

"Don't shoot your load all at once, lad. This isn't a sprint."

But the extended burst of flame had done its job; the blob had retreated completely and Wiggo could see all the way down the alleyway. It led to a flight of steps, down into a basement bar. The bar door was open and the whole area around it glistened and shimmered in an oily rainbow aurora.

"Maybe it fancies a pint," Wilkins said as they ran towards the steps.

"Well, we've got something in common after all then," Wiggo replied.

There was a series of crashes and thuds from down in the bar, The Coal Hole Wiggo saw from the sign, as if furniture was being thrown around in a rage.

"Maybe the beer's shite," he said. "Let's go and see."

Wiggo took the lead as they went down into the bar. They went inside just in time to see the last of the blob pull itself away through a door right at the back, leaving behind a glistening oily residue over the whole room.

"After it," he shouted, and ran forward.

The doorway led away down a flight of stone steps to what was obviously a beer cellar. It was pitch black down there. Wiggo switched on his helmet light and leaned in for a look.

A pulsating mass of protoplasm surged up towards him out of the darkness.

Wiggo tried to find the trigger of the flame-thrower but his finger had slipped off it, and he had no time to look down; the thing was almost on him. He said a silent prayer and waited for oblivion, only to find himself thrust roughly to one side. He felt a flash of heat as Wilkins pulled the trigger, too close for comfort, saw a flash, red then yellow, then Wilkins was screaming.

Wiggo rolled to one side and got up to see the private lying at the open doorway. A quick look showed there was only blackness down the stairwell. He sent a two second burst of flame down anyway, just in case, then he had to turn his attention to the private. The cost of saving Wiggo's life had been a wash of the protoplasm across the front of his legs. His trousers were melting against his flesh and the lad was screaming blue murder. Wiggo helped him shuck out of the trousers, trying to keep his hands well away from any of the oily residue. Clear of the melting material, Wilkins kicked it away into the black stairwell. Blisters were already raised along the length of both his legs from thigh to ankle. The skin looked tight, red and angry.

Wiggo switched on his radio.

"Cap, you there? We need medical attention and we need it fast."

Banks came back immediately.

"We're coming to you. Thirty seconds."

Wilkins grimaced, managed a smile and looked up at Wiggo.

"You make one single comment about getting into my pants and I'm going to have to kill you."

Wiggo looked around then smiled back.

"We're in a basement bar in the center of London. What else was I supposed to do?"

Banks and Davies arrived seconds later and Davies set about doing what he could for the other private. A minute later he looked up.

"We need to get him out of here and into a burns unit, fast," he said. "The quicker we get him there, the easier the rehab's going to be."

Wiggo could hear the sirens in the road above, close now.

"Sounds like the cavalry's here. Let's go."

They carted Wilkins up into the open and were lucky to almost walk straight into a team of first responders who took one look at the lad and whisked him away, siren blaring and lights flashing.

The captain must have seen the shake in Wiggo's hands. He lit a cigarette for both of them before passing one over.

"Here's where you tell me what the fuck just happened," he said while Wiggo took in a lungful of smoke and let it out slowly.

-WIGGO-

Wiggo brought the captain up to speed, and in return Wiggo found out that the injured they'd brought up out of the tube station were also on their way to hospital.

"Will they make it?" Wiggo asked, and got a see-saw wave of a hand in response.

Wiggo finished the cigarette.

"We'd best have a look down in yon cellar," he said. "The bugger might be lurking down there."

"Are you sure you're up for it, Sarge?"

"Aye. The lad saved my life. The least I can do is make sure I was worth it."

The road was a hive of activity, mainly first responders, firemen and police, all trying to make sense of what they were being asked to clean up. Several of them eyed the flame-throwers the squad were wearing, but mostly they were all too busy with the wounded and dying, of which there were many.

"We need to get this fucker, Cap," Wiggo said. "It's like an all you can eat buffet for it around here."

"And it went down into the cellar?"

"Aye, and it came up again like a bat out of hell, so we best go careful."

Banks led Wiggo and Davies back to the alleyway where all three stopped and looked down into the darkness of the bar.

"You still packing?" Banks asked Wiggo.

"Got enough for one long spurt then I'm done, as the bishop said to the actress. But the lad's tanks are down there by the cellar door; there's probably six seconds in them too if we cart them along with us."

"Let's see what there is to see first."

The walls of the bar glistened with the oily residue, and there was much more of it splashed around the cellar door. Wiggo stepped forward gingerly and looked down, seeing only bare stairs. He emptied his tanks down the stairwell then swapped for the ones Wilkins had left behind. Banks moved towards the stairs but Wiggo stepped in front of him.

"This is my shout, Cap. For the lad."

Banks nodded and stood aside. Wiggo went back to the top of the stairwell and looked down into the blackness. His legs said no but his brain said yes, and these days that was the stronger muscle. He headed down, ensuring that he kept his finger over the wand's trigger.

Nothing attacked him on the stairs. When they arrived in the beer cellar, they saw that the thing had been busy. The metal barrels were thrown against the cellar walls; the older wooden caskets of real ale were all in the center of the area, empty and partially melted down into a pile of bubbling slime on the floor.

"I was right," Wiggo muttered to himself. "It did fancy a pint."

The cellar was a long narrow one, receding away into darkness ahead of them. When Wiggo swung his headlight in that direction the glistening residue reflected a rainbow aurora back at him. He stepped gingerly around the bubbling slime beneath the beer barrels and headed along the length of the cellar. The residue glowed more strongly the farther in he got.

"It went this way," he said. "Go canny in here, lads. I've seen this bugger's moves; it can come at you fast."

That proved prophetic. Just as Wiggo was starting to think they were heading for a dead end his headlights caught a heap of tumbled stone ahead, with a darker-still entrance beyond.

"This is where it got in," he said, realising too late that his voice came too loud in the enclosed space. And in immediate response a four foot thick pseudopod snaked out of the hole, coming directly at him.

"Not this time, fucker," Wiggo said and pulled the trigger, sending a wash of flame over the attacking blob. It sizzled and boiled and beat a hasty retreat even after Wiggo let go of the trigger. Beyond the hole he saw something larger shift in the shadows.

"I see you," he whispered and strode forward, clambering over the fallen stones to look into the blackness. A shimmering aura filled what looked to be a tunnel melted down and away from the cellar into deeper parts. The bulk of the blob was at the range of Wiggo's vision, retreating fast.

"Oh no you don't. You're mine, you bastard."

He leapt after it, vaguely aware that the captain was shouting at his back. He paid it no heed; his blood was up, and he had a debt to repay. He sent another two second burst after the retreating beast, yelling in triumph when he saw it char and roil.

The blob went down seeking refuge in the depths. Wiggo ran after it.

Wiggo threw all caution to the wind in his pursuit. The only thing that saved him from tumbling arse over tit was the fact that the going underfoot was as perfectly smooth as the walls, melted then fused again into almost glass-like flatness. The jerky light from his headset showed him only glimpses of the blob, not quite enough to allow him the luxury of pulling the trigger, for he knew he only had three seconds of fuel remaining at best. Given the size of the beast he was going to need more than that; he hoped the Cap and Davies would be with him in time to watch his back.

"Where's fucking Steve McQueen when you need him?" he muttered.

The descent continued, the tunnel slowly but surely levelling out so that it didn't feel quite so much like a headlong rush to hell. He'd been watching his feet and looked up, in the nick of time to avoid running directly into a wall of protoplasm that filled the tunnel just yards below him. He deliberately fell on his arse, feeling the jar all the way up his spine, and scrambled backward pumping his legs, his feet an inch, two inches, three inches from the quivering blob.

He was too close, far too close to risk the flame-thrower; the blowback would in all likelihood turn him into a crispy critter. He reached with his free hand for his flak jacket, his fingers falling on one of his stun grenades. To use it would be almost as risky as the flames; it was liable to burst his eardrums and maybe also blind him at this range. But the blob was coming up the tunnel towards him, getting close to the tips of his boots again. He heard the captain yell somewhere above him, but had no time to reply, no time to think. He pulled the pin, lobbed the stun grenade and threw himself aside, face down, hands over his ears.

The expected explosion never came. There was a dull 'crump' then a whoosh, like water going down a drain, then the captain was there, turning Wiggo over to check him out.

"What just happened?" Wiggo said.

"It swallowed your whiz-bang. That's what happened. The blast went off inside it, and it took off like a scalded cat, away down the tunnel. I think you gave it a fright."

"No' nearly half as much as the one it gave me," Wiggo said, getting unsteadily to his feet. "Sorry, Cap. I let the blood rush to my head."

"Better there than in your bollocks," Banks replied. "Come on. Let's finish this fucker off while we've got it on the run."

Wiggo followed Banks and Davies down the tunnel.

There was no sign of the blob.

-WIGGO-

The tunnel had almost levelled out. Wiggo tried to mentally map where they might be now; he thought they might be heading south and west, but his knowledge of London wasn't good enough to imagine what might now be on top of them. After five more minutes they came to a junction. A wider tunnel containing a long disused narrow-gauge railway line stretched away left and right, but the glistening residue wasn't visible on the walls in either direction. Directly opposite them the melted, smooth tunnel continued. There was dim light in the distance somewhere ahead. Banks led them towards it.

They emerged onto a platform at Charing Cross tube station. There was a train stopped halfway out of the tunnel to their left. It hadn't made it to the platform, and neither had its passengers. What was left of them was little more than pink sludge on the rails, on the platform and around the stairwell leading to the lights. Wiggo couldn't even begin to calculate how many might be dead, but guessed it was somewhere north of a hundred. Everything, rails, carriage and walls was covered in the glistening oily residue. Nothing moved and there was no sound except for the hiss of static in Wiggo's earpiece.

"Fuck me, Cap," he said. "What's going on here? Where's the rescue teams?"

He saw Banks tap at his own earpiece and shake his head.

"Your guess is as good as mine, Sarge. This is a full on fucking disaster."

The carnage was all on the opposite side of the rails from where they stood and that was just fine by Wiggo. He followed Banks to the right. The tunnel in that direction appeared to be empty of either train or blob, although it too had the same glistening residue coating its sides.

"This thing's got fucking everywhere," Davies whispered.

"Aye," the captain replied. "Either it's bigger than we think, or it's faster than we've seen so far."

"Or maybe it's both," Wiggo added, and wished he hadn't thought of it.

They got ten yards along the platform before they realized they'd made a big, possibly fatal, mistake. The tunnel ahead of them filled rapidly with protoplasm, as did the stairwell that came down to the platform near it, a wave of the translucent matrix sluggishly washing down the steps. When Wiggo turned to head back the way they'd come he saw that the opposite end of the tunnel was also filling, the blob oozing around and over the tube train carriages. Not only that, more of it was pushing through from the tunnel that they had descended.

"Bugger me," Wiggo said. "We're going to need bigger flame-throwers."

"How the fuck did it get behind us?" Davies said.

"It oozed," Wiggo replied. "It's what it is, it's what it does. What now, Cap?"

As he spoke he saw a tremor, like a ripple, pass across the surface of the protoplasm. The reason came to him all at one, a combination of old George's journal, the screaming people on the Aldwych station platform, the way it had come at him in the cellar of the bar, and the effect of the whiz-bang. He leaned in close to the captain and whispered.

"It keys on sound."

Banks nodded to show that he understood and led Wiggo and Davies quickly and quietly across the rails towards the only exit available to them: the stairwell on the far side. In the short time it took them to reach it, the protoplasm filled up half the chamber and was showing no signs of slowing. The matrix was almost pink in hue, with chunks of red embedded in it that Wiggo didn't care to look at too closely. The clearer parts flowed faster than the more pinkish areas, but all of it moved, flowing and sinuous. There was something almost hypnotic about it, like watching lava flow from a volcanic vent.

Wiggo had to force himself to drag his gaze away.

The captain stopped them at the entrance to the stairwell. They had been walking in pink slime, something else Wiggo was trying hard not to think about.

"It's too big for us to handle," Banks said. "But we can't let it get up top; imagine if this lot all got out at once among the tourists. So let's see if we can slow it down. Let's see how it handles more than one whiz-bang at a time."

They each took a stun-grenade in hand then, on the captain's order, lobbed them high and hard into the main mass of the thing. They were away and running for the stairwell before the triple blast went off, not quite simultaneously, with a roar and flash that lit the stairwell up then left dancing light in Wiggo's eyes for long seconds afterwards. An open lift door beckoned them inside and Wiggo made for it, only to be stopped by Banks.

"Too much noise," the captain whispered, and headed for the stairs. Wiggo looked up. They were at the foot of a stopped escalator stairway that seemed to go on forever, up into darkness high above. He turned back to look at the exit out onto the platform. There was no sign of the blob in the small part of the chamber he could see, but he wasn't going to venture closer to check. When Banks started up the escalator stairs, Wiggo let Davies follow first then started up at their back.

The efforts of the day were starting to tell on them and they took the stairs slowly. After twenty steps Wiggo was grunting with exertion, the weight of the flame-thrower dragging at him, causing him to lean forward lest he be pitched over backwards down the stairwell. There was no noise from either below or above, disconcerting here in the center of one of the world's major cities, made more so by the fact that there was still no sign of rescue services despite the obvious mayhem that had been wrought in the station below.

Banks brought them to a grateful halt on a landing at the top where they had a smoke in silence. A tiled tunnel snaked away ahead of them. Wiggo chanced a look back down the stairwell. There was no sign that the thing was following them. He was about to say a silent prayer of thanks when the area echoed and rumbled with sound. He heard the 'ting' of a bell, the swish of closing doors then the lift started to ascend. Seconds later his headlight lit up a wash of protoplasm coming in off the platform; if their whiz-bangs had scared it, it hadn't stayed that way for long. It was already a foot deep in the floor below, and getting deeper by the second.

Wiggo got his last two stun-grenades from his jacket, pulled the pins and threw them, bouncing away, down the escalator.

"Fire in the hole."

The blast lit the whole landing up and the echoes rang in his ears. The lift continued to ascend.

"Best get moving," Wiggo said. "I think it's still hungry."

The three men headed into the tiled tunnel, the groans and creaks of the lift still clearly audible.

-WIGGO-

The corridor took a long slow curve to their left and after ten paces or so Wiggo looked back to see they were now cut off from a view of the landing behind them. That led to his mind's eye furnishing him with pictures of the blob oozing up the escalator, filling the shaft with its bulk, more and more of it coming out from the platform to chase the sound of the lift.

"Can we get a move on here, Cap," he said. "My arse is getting itchy."

They put on as much of a spurt as they could manage. Wiggo heard noise, not from behind but in front of them, and seconds later they came to the end of the curve and onto a larger open landing, a junction point for the various platforms. There was another tunnel exit opposite them and escalators going down to their left and up to their right. The one going up was the source of the noise; it was in operation. The one going down wasn't working but they heard the machinery creak and groan as if it was straining against something. Wiggo stepped over and looked down. The escalator was choked with protoplasm to almost a third of the way up and the blob was flowing swiftly towards the men.

"Going to need a hand here, lads," Wiggo said. At the sound the protoplasm surged, a tube of protoplasm filling the shaft below from escalator to roof as it came. Banks and Davies were almost immediately at Wiggo's side, pulling grenades from their jackets. It was coming so fast they weren't going to get time to throw them. Wiggo stepped forward, aimed his wand, pulled the trigger and sent the full contents of his fire extinguisher down to meet the rising blob. Fire washed back up the shaft, so much that they had to move back quickly. The blob kept coming even as its surface bubbled and boiled under the flame.

"Up the stairs, quick," Banks shouted. Wiggo didn't wait, he turned and ran for the upward moving escalator. Seconds later everything went up in light and noise as the captain and Davies threw their grenades. Then all three of them were on the escalator, bounding upwards faster than the moving steps. They didn't stop until they reached the top and looked out over a deserted ticket hall.

Banks looked back down the escalator shaft.

"All clear, for now. But I don't think we should hang about."

The ticket hall showed signs that there had been a hasty exit made through it. Handbags, briefcases, umbrellas and discarded shoes lay strewn on the floor, and there was blood on the turnstiles and ticket machines. To Wiggo's bemusement there was still no sign of any first response units.

"Where the fuck is everybody?"

He turned to the captain to look for a reply and saw that Banks had his finger at his ear, listening to a call that Wiggo wasn't privy to. Wiggo lit a smoke while waiting and saw Davies light up on the far side of the captain.

The call took a few minutes and Banks' face was grave when it was done.

"They've abandoned central London and called a general curfew," he said. "We're to fall back to High Holborn where there's a command center set up, and wait for further instruction."

"A general curfew in central London? Can they do that? It must be a shitload of people."

"Not as many as there were," Banks said grimly. "The death toll is in the hundreds, and still rising."

They moved quickly through the empty ticket hall and up another functioning escalator that took them into Charing Cross railway station. It was as empty as the tube station had been and showed all the signs of the same hasty retreat. Wiggo was still struggling to grasp the enormity of the situation as they walked out of the station and looked out over the main road. Abandoned vehicles; cars, trucks and the distinctive red double-deckers blocked the road in both directions as far as they could see. Everything was deadly quiet and still.

"There's not even a bloody pigeon," Wiggo whispered. "This is fucking mental."

"Bigger and faster than we thought, remember?" Banks said. 'Let's just get back to base and see what's what. We can check up on young Wilkins from there, too."

Wiggo had little sense of where they were; London was an alien city to him. But Banks seemed to know where he was going. The three of them moved quickly, taking a series of alleys and side streets until they emerged in a spot Wiggo recognised from movies and TV. But Covent Garden had never looked like this before.

Bodies, some little more than skeletons, others partially digested and fused like molten candles, lay strewn everywhere. The protoplasm still fed in places, having oozed up through grates and manholes to pool in festering, bubbling puddles. Wiggo watched in horror as a body flowed past, tugged along, arm waving as if in goodbye as it went down and away into a sewer.

"Burn it, Cap," he whispered. "For pity's sake, burn the fucker."

"Sorry, Sarge, no can do. We're under orders not to engage."

Wiggo shook his flame-thrower, hoping to find enough fuel with which to disobey, but he was totally dry, and the look on Banks' face told him not to push it.

The captain was looking out over the grisly scene with a fixed stare.

"For once I agree with you though, Sarge. Orders or no orders, this isn't right. We can't just leave it at this." He turned to Davies. "Light it up. It's all we can do for these poor fuckers."

Davies and the captain sent washes of flame over the esplanade and buildings of the interior courtyard. It all burned: blob, people and buildings. They watched as black smoke rose in a funereal plume then Wiggo put his head down, concentrated on looking at his feet, and followed the captain north into Long Acre. It was full of discarded vehicles but, thankfully, no more melting dead.

In contrast to the quiet streets to the south and west, the High Holborn junction was a hive of activity. The captain headed off towards a truck that looked like the locus to find someone to report to, leaving Wiggo and Davies to divest themselves of the flame-throwers and enjoy a most welcome smoke break. There was a large crowd gathered behind the northern edge of the control barrier, and Wiggo wasn't surprised to see old George standing there waving his walking stick to attract his attention. Wiggo walked over.

"How's tricks, auld yin?"

"Better now for seeing you still with us," George replied, then leaned forward conspiratorially. "We need to talk. There's something I haven't told you. Something that's not in the journal. It's supposed to be an official secret, but I think we're long past time for all that bollocks, don't you? It's important. Do you fancy a pint?"

-GEORGE-

"It was in '68, at the height of the Cold War," George began. He, Wiggo and Davies were back in the Kingsway Tavern bar, empty save for them and the obsequious barman who'd just got in a round of beer and cheese toasties. "The Prof and I had been quiet for years. He was working away in some research which was proving boring but restful while I had moved on to Whitehall and some of the more bureaucratic warrens of power. I expected to be doing the same for a while in a long wind down to eventual retirement and obscurity. Then I got a call I didn't expect, from the MOD no less, summoning me to an urgent meeting. You can imagine my surprise when I found that the Prof was already there when I entered.

"We weren't given any chance to catch up on old times. A man in a suit as grey as his face made the Prof sign the Official Secrets Act-I was already a signatory-then we were asked some general questions about what we had been working on since 'the problem in Oxford'. Only after they were satisfied that we weren't likely to be Iron Curtain agents looking to infiltrate the British Government were we let in on the reason we had been called for.

"'We have a sample,' the grey suit said. 'Not from Oxford, but from the British Antarctic Survey. From your descriptions of the nature of the thing you encountered, we believe it to be similar, if not identical. As the only two people around who saw it properly back then, we need your input on this.'

"'I'll tell you my input right here and now,' the Prof said. 'Pour some molar acid on the bloody thing and walk away. Any other path of action is pure folly.'

"The Prof's protestations washed off the grey suit, water off a duck's back. We were taken down into the bowels of Whitehall to an old brick bunker; I'd heard rumors of it but never really believed it existed until then, so I was even more amazed when we went down another stairwell and onto a train platform.

"'Churchill had this put in during the war,' we were told. 'All very hush hush. Uses an old Royal Mail line but he had that suborned to his will and we've had use of it ever since.'

"'Where does it go?' I asked.

"'To where we keep the stuff we don't want the public to see,' he replied, then would say no more."

"All I know is the train took us east, and at one point I caught a glimpse of a tube train hurtling past in an adjoining tunnel. Somewhere to the east of Charing Cross under the Embankment would be my guess as to our destination. It was a warren of bricked up corridors and even older old-stone chambers. I wouldn't have been at all surprised to find some of it dated back to Roman times.

"The MOD had a laboratory of sorts set up down there, at the end of a corridor of closed metal doors we were not allowed to inspect. As it was, the laboratory itself was bad enough. When they said they had a 'sample', I'd thought of something in a test tube. The tank they had it in was ten by four by three and it sloshed around inside as if driven by some unseen tidal force. I recognised it immediately of course; it was the same stuff, or as near as made no damned difference.

"The suit wanted to know whether we recognised it, but I had some questions of my own first.

"'Where was it found?'

"He hummed and hawed, but finally answered.

"'In a lake under nearly a mile of ice. We've been trying out some experimental drilling techniques and...'

"'Let me guess,' the Prof said sarcastically. 'This stuff came up your drill bit and started feeding. I watch the news. Scientists 'missing in bad weather' the report said, didn't it? Missing, presumed eaten is my guess.'

"The suit had the good grace to look embarrassed.

"'Look, just tell me, is it the same material? That's what we're here to find out.'

"'It might be what you're here to find out,' the Prof said. 'But now you've got me interested. Why is it here at all? Why didn't it just get dumped back under the ice?'

"'That's classified information, I'm afraid.'

"'Classified my bloody arse. You're the MOD. You're planning to weaponize it, aren't you? What have you been doing? Giving it treats? Or is pain more efficient? I bet you've tried just about everything. What's working best? Acid or fire?'

"The MOD man sputtered and went red in the face. It didn't suit him.

"'Someone's been talking.'

"'No,' the Prof said softly. 'You're just not used to someone with brains around here.'

"He pointed at the still-sloshing tank of protoplasm.

"'Here's some free advice from the smartest man in the room. Destroy it now. Right now, or you'll regret it later.'

"I tried to add my voice of reason to the Prof's. But the suit wasn't about to listen to a provincial professor and his erstwhile assistant. He was MOD. He was following orders. We got marched out of there pronto and twenty minutes later were out on the street blinking in the sun.

"The Prof was full of bluster, talking about going to the papers with the story, crazy talk that would have got us both locked away in a dark place for the duration. So I took him to a pub and poured beer and scotch into him until he calmed down and saw sense.

"We never talked about it again, but I know I kept a closer eye on the London papers after that, and I'm sure he did too."

-WIGGO-

George sat back and finished off the last third of his pint, calling for another.

"You think they kept it down there, don't you?" Wiggo said. "Kept it and grew it and then, somehow, recently, it got out?"

George nodded as the barman returned with another round for the three of them.

"That's exactly what I think. And I think if you go buggering about underground just to the east of Charing Cross you'll find the proof of what I've just told you."

"So where does that get us?"

"Pretty much nowhere, apart from one thing," George said, taking a long sip of beer then wiping foam from his lip. "What if it's territorial? What if it stays close to home?"

Wiggo was still trying to process George's story when the barman switched on the flat screen TV above the bar.

"You need to see this. It's fucking wild."

The picture showed a familiar scene; the view from the National Gallery balustrade across Trafalgar Square and down Whitehall to Big Ben. What wasn't familiar was the total lack of people- and the bubbling, oozing, flowing mass of protoplasm that filled the square to a depth of six feet or more. There were things embedded in the matrix, all too human in shape for some, smaller, almost globular for others. Wiggo realized what he must be looking at.

"The fucker ate all the bloody pigeons."

The camera zoomed in to show a finger of protoplasm leaving the square and heading down Whitehall towards the Cenotaph. A death toll count ran along the bottom of the screen. It was now over a thousand. The camera switched to other well-known city scenes; a deserted Piccadilly Circus where the only sign of life was the ever-shifting advertising billboards meant for consumers rather than the consumed who lay in a festering puddle around Eros' uncaring feet.

Oxford Street had been spared the ravages of the blob but lay quiet and empty save for a single rebel parading its length wearing an 'The End is Nigh' sandwich board. The picture moved to Westminster Bridge, where a minister was being interviewed. The nervous looking man kept casting looks over his shoulder, past Big Ben towards the Cenotaph. Wiggo guessed his arse was getting itchy. The last shot was along the Mall towards the empty forecourt of Buckingham Palace. There was no flag showing; the royals had long since been packed off to the safety of Windsor Castle.

Their viewing was interrupted by the arrival of Captain Banks.

"I guessed I'd find you here," he said. "Finish up those beers, lads. We're going back in."

Over the next few minutes Banks relayed what he knew, which wasn't much more than they'd just seen on the TV, with the added fact that the intention was to encircle the beast and herd it somewhere where the newly arrived tankers of acid could be deployed. That 'somewhere' was yet to be identified.

"I might be able to help with that," George said and tapped the side of his nose. "I've got contacts who've got contacts, if you know what I mean?"

"And Wilkins? Any news on the lad?"

"Safely ensconced in the burns unit, getting treatment and fighting off the advances of the nurses, both male and female," Burns said with a smile. "I spoke to him. He'll be fine, eventually."

Wiggo felt relief wash over him. Banks made ready to leave but Wiggo stopped him.

"One more thing, Cap," he said. "The auld yin here thinks he knows where that beastie calls home."

"It's just a theory," George said.

"Aye, so's gravity," Banks answered laconically. "Let's have it."

Wiggo gave him the potted version. Banks nodded at the end of the tale.

"Sounds plausible," he said. "But it's a moot point right now. There's a couple of hundred squaddies armed with flame-throwers about to descend into the sewers and tube tunnels; we're just going to be three of many."

"Where do we start from?" Wiggo asked, hoping it might be somewhere nearer Charing Cross. That hope was quickly dashed.

"We're here already," the captain said. "We go down yon manhole out at the junction and take it from there."

As they were leaving, old George was getting

another pint in for himself. He tapped at his ear.

"I'll be in touch," he said.

The three of them spent the next few minutes getting kitted up again; fresh cylinders for the flame-throwers, new batteries in the headlight helmets and half a dozen stun grenades each in the webbing of their flak jackets.

"So we go in mob-handed and try to get a big fucking blobby thing to go where we want it to go? That's the plan?" Wiggo said.

"Yep," Banks said and grinned. "Why, you got a better one, Sarge?"

Wiggo was thinking that maybe investigating the tunnels under Charing Cross would be a better idea, but kept his mouth shut. The captain had his orders, which meant Wiggo had his orders too, and he'd learned a long time ago to take that seriously.

"Lay on, MacDuff," he said. "And don't spare the horses."

It was starting to get dark again by the time they went down into the sewer. They had spent the day subsiding on beer, fags and cheese toasties but to be fair, it wasn't the worst day they'd had on that front, not by a long chalk. The weight of the flame-thrower dragged heavy on his shoulders but Wiggo knew his limits; he was good for a few hours more yet. The crash, when it came, was likely to be spectacular though.

They went through the sewer to where the smooth-sided tunnel led down and away south.

"Which way, Cap?" Wiggo asked.

"One's as good as another," Banks replied. "I guess we blunder about until we find something, then try to make sure it heads in the right direction, wherever the fuck that might be."

It sounded like the captain wasn't exactly enamoured with his orders. Wiggo took that as a chance to take the initiative and started off down the tunnel, retracing their steps from before. Banks and Davies followed, neither of them contradicting Wiggo's choice.

He led down to where the tunnel joined the old sewer then went right, heading back towards where they'd followed the screams to Aldwych earlier. Wiggo might not know too much about London geography, but he had a good memory, and this was also in the general direction of where George thought they needed to go, a win all round.

They were stopped by a crackle in their headsets.

"Contact," someone shouted. "Leicester Square. I repeat, Leicester Square. All teams converge."

"Might as well tell us to converge on bloody Glasgow for all the good it does down here," Banks muttered at Wiggo's back.

"What do we do, Cap?"

"Well we can't get there from here, not soon anyway," Banks said. "Keep going the way we're going, Sarge. It's in the general direction, that's the best we can do at the moment."

Their earpieces crackled again. A frantic voice came over the air.

"My God, it's fucking huge!"

There was a single, short-lived scream, then only

static until another voice, more authoritative, came through.

"Leicester Square. Converge on Leicester Square."

-WIGGO-

They went down and were soon at the grille that led out onto Aldwych station. There was only static in their earpieces now, and they didn't know whether it was because they were under too much earth or, a worse thought, there was no one left to broadcast. Those thoughts were dispelled quickly when they looked out over the disused station to see a large pool of the protoplasm oozing over the rails. It covered an area maybe twenty yards long by five wide, appeared to be moving independently and wasn't connected to any larger mass of the thing at either end.

Banks pulled them back to the other side of the grille and leaned in close.

"The bugger's calving," he said. "This changes everything. It could be anywhere."

The captain tried to reach someone, anyone, on his radio. Wiggo saw by the look on his face he had no joy.

Wiggo chanced a look out at the moving blob. It was travelling away from them to their right heading for the mouth of the tube tunnel. He pointed.

"Charing Cross is that way. Right? So what if auld George is right? This could be it heading home to its mammie."

"That's about as sensible as anything else I've

heard today," Banks replied. "What do you want to do, Wiggo? It's your shout."

Wiggo went with his gut. They kept a close eye on the patch of blob as it travelled along the rails and vanished into the right hand tunnel. Wiggo waited for another minute after that, then motioned for the others to follow.

Wiggo avoided the rails on general principle although the blob had flowed easily enough over them so there was no way they could be live. His helmet light lit up a trail of glistening slime that was easy to follow, leading directly off down the tracks. Wherever the thing was going, it was going fast.

His earpiece squawked again.

"Shaftesbury Avenue. It's under Shaftesbury Avenue."

"No, we have it here," somebody else said. "Beneath Admiralty Arch."

"Leicester Square. It's still in Leicester Square station," a panicked voice came in. "It's right here with me and I'm out of fuel. Oh God, won't somebody come?"

That call ended with more screams, more static.

"I think the big plan's in trouble, Cap," Wiggo said softly. "You still okay following me?"

"I trust your gut more than I trust the brass, Wiggo. Lead on."

They went ten more yards. The glistening trail stopped, having disappeared on the far side of the rails. When Wiggo stepped over to investigate he found a small drain, no more than six inches in diameter, coated in glimmering slime. Wherever the thing had gone, they weren't going to be able to follow.

"I need your help with the geography, Cap," Wiggo said. "We're in Aldwych, heading for Charing Cross. That means we're going due west?"

"Just about," Banks replied.

"Aye, that's what I thought. We need to be going south of here, towards the embankment, that's what the auld lad said."

"All well and good, Wiggo," Banks replied. "And that's the way the beastie here is going. But unless you've just lost a fuckload of weight, there's no way we're going after it."

Wiggo looked along the track in both directions, and just that act brought him the answer.

"Rails. The wee railway. George said they used that in '68. That was next to Charing Cross station, wasn't it?"

"Aye. But to get there, we have to go through and down yon escalators again. You ken what we left there."

Wiggo nodded.

"But we don't have to go that way. This line goes to Charing Cross, somewhere. We follow it, then find our way to the right platform avoiding all the shite up top. Easy peasy."

"Lemon squeezy," Banks finished. "As I said, it's your shout. We're off the reservation and disobeying direct orders already. Might as well make the most of it."

Wiggo led the squad out.

All he knew was that he was heading in the

direction of Charing Cross; the rest of the plan was still vague in his head. But fate handed him a lifeline a minute later when they came to a side tunnel heading away and down to their left, an old red-brick affair that looked like it hadn't been used for years. There were grooves in the ground where rails had been but they too had been taken up years ago. The thing that got Wiggo interested was the faded writing in foot-high letters on the wall just inside the corridor. It was almost too faint to read, but he made it out well enough.

Royal Mail.

There was no sign of any glistening aurora in this new tunnel; Wiggo didn't know whether to take that as a good sign or not, but it was going in the right direction to satisfy the map he had built in his head, so he headed that way, with the captain and Davies at his back. His finger instinctively found the trigger of the flame-thrower wand. His spidey-sense was tingling now, adrenaline pumping, all his nerves on edge and ready for action.

He almost leapt in the air when someone screamed in the radio earpiece, a long wail of terror that was cut short by a blast of static then silence. Banks spoke up at Wiggo's back.

"You sure about this, lad?"

"Nope. But my gut is. And remember, it keys on sound. Best keep quiet until we know what's what."

The captain looked like he might reprimand Wiggo for exceeding his privileges, then smiled thinly and nodded, slotting in behind when they moved on.

The radio in his ear crackled again.

"Fall back. Fall back. Regroup in High Holborn. I repeat…"

The repeat never came. There was another hiss of static, then just silence. Wiggo didn't bother checking with the captain. He continued to head deeper into the tunnel.

His hunch proved right after ten minutes of descent when they came to an opening onto a long-disused platform. There was no train in the station, no sign of life, but there was plenty of the oily residue and a shimmering aurora hung over the whole site. Electric light poured through on the far side of the station from an open metal doorway. Wiggo motioned he was heading that way and headed over, the others at his heels, all three with their fingers hovering on the wand triggers.

The door was being held open by the partially digested remains of two bodies, little more than scraps and skeleton and one fully preserved shoe, leather, brogue and bloody expensive to Wiggo's admittedly untrained eye.

"Whatever happened here was fairly recent," he whispered. "Eyes open, lads, we're going in."

The corridor inside was better maintained than the platform outside. The brickwork had been relatively recently whitewashed, the light fittings were modern, almost too bright after their tramping about in the gloom, and they passed metal doors, all firmly shut, all fitted with state of the art security locking. Below door-handle level was a different matter though; the blob had flowed through here and left its glistening trail over floor and walls, although Wiggo was unable to tell as yet whether it had been on its way in or on its way out.

The answer to that came at the end of the long corridor. Here they found another open door, more half-eaten bodies propping it open. Wiggo stepped gingerly over the stinking mess and into the room beyond. It was a larger, higher-ceilinged space that had been a laboratory of sorts judging by the computers, spectrometers and sealed work spaces around the walls. The only thing of any great age in the room was a huge, Second-World-War vintage radio set on the wall nearest the door.

"Broadsword calling Danny Boy," Wiggo muttered as he stepped into the center of the room.

The far wall was dominated by a glass tank, or rather, the remnants of one, for the glass had shattered and was scattered among the debris and slime on the floor.

Wiggo stepped over another body, little more than a rib-cage and legs, and gave the tank a closer look. It was fed from a wide pipe at the rear that led away into darkness. The walls of the pipe glistened with slime.

"They studied it in here," Wiggo said softly, waving at the remnants of the tank. "But I think it lived through there."

He pointed at the pipe.

Banks nodded in agreement, then looked startled when Wiggo climbed up into the shattered tank.

"Where do you think you're going, lad?"

"With respect, Cap, we didnae come all this way to look at some broken glass and the thing's dinner.

We need to know what's through there. I don't like it, I'm sure you don't like it... but what else can we do?"

"Do I get a vote?" Davies said behind them.

"No," Wiggo and Banks answered in unison, and just like that any tension there had been was washed away as all three of them laughed.

"Okay, Wiggo," Banks said. "We'll do this one your way. That way I can blame it all on you when it goes tits-up."

"Same as it ever was, Cap," Wiggo replied, and headed for the pipe.

-WIGGO-

He picked his way over more broken glass and stood in front of the gaping maw of the pipe, staring into the blackness before switching on his headlight. He let out a sigh of relief when nothing surged out at him and his light showed only glistening walls leading away to darker shadows beyond. The air tasted dank and stagnant, like an old well left too long without fresh water. The pipe was just about tall and wide enough to mean he could sidle through it without getting on his hands and knees, so there was that at least to be thankful for, as he hadn't relished getting too close to the slimy residue.

He started in, cautiously, and heard the others make their way across the bottom of the tank behind him. Five yards in the pipe opened out into what felt like a much larger area. He played his light around and saw it was another bricked up area, an old storeroom of some kind, almost ten yards in circumference with a concreted over exit directly across from him and a high vaulted brickwork arched ceiling overhead. The floor appeared to be covered in a shimmering oily rainbow and when he stepped forward he sloshed in a viscous fluid that almost covered the toes and heel of his boots.

There was no sign of the blob but Wiggo took things slowly; he'd seen enough monster movies to know that this was usually the point where our heroes got their arses kicked. His headlight picked out something on the floor ahead, a cluster of things, oval shaped, like American footballs stood on end. Wiggo had seen this movie too and kept well back.

"Got something you need to see here, Cap," he said, trying not to let a quiver show in his voice. Banks and Davies came to his side and all three shone their lights on the cluster. They didn't look like eggs so much as some kind of spore, thick skinned, almost scaly and covered in rough spiny hairs like some kind of exotic fruit.

"Is that how it reproduces?" Davies whispered.

"Possibly," Banks said. "Whatever they are, we don't fuck with them. We need to get some scientists down here."

"Aye, good luck with that, Cap. I think those poor buggers out in the doorways were the scientists."

"I'm open to ideas, Wiggo,"

"Aye, well I don't think you're going to like this one," Wiggo replied. "Can we go back to the lab first though, I'm gasping for a fag and would rather not light up in here."

Once back in the lab, Wiggo passed round the cigarettes and they all lit up before he spoke again.

"Auld George thought the beastie might be territorial, didn't he?" He didn't wait for a reply. "If so, it stands to reason this is home and yon things in there that we just found? They're its family."

"Sounds feasible," Banks said. "How does that help us?"

"From what we've seen so far, if we hurt any bit

of this thing, it all reacts, right?"

The others nodded in agreement.

"And it keys on noise, right?"

More nods.

"So what if we, noisily, burn those fucking spores down into the brickwork? Do you think that might get its attention?"

"Aye, that'll work, right enough. But your plan only gets us so far, Wiggo. We get the beastie to come to us, so far so sound. But I'm far from convinced we've got the firepower to take all of it down. Yon bugger's fucking massive."

"I'm working on that," Wiggo said. "We need some way of getting the acid out of yon tankers up top, and down here where it might be of some use to us."

"Any idea how?"

"Not a fucking clue, Cap. But I ken an auld man who might. Can we get H.Q. on the blower?"

Banks tried his radio, but Wiggo knew from his expression he was getting nowhere. His gaze fell on the wall-sized radio by the door.

"What about old-school? Do you think Danny Boy's on any frequency yon thing can muster?"

Davies stepped over and had a look then smiled.

"Give me ten minutes with her and I'll have her purring."

"As the bishop said to the actress."

Banks and Wiggo had another smoke while Davies set to tinkering, Banks keeping an eye on the doorway, Wiggo watching the pipeline into the dark storeroom.

"You really think the auld man can help us?" Banks said.

"He got us a pint, in London, long outside opening hours," Wiggo said with a grin. "I think he's capable of just about anything. He's got contacts on the inside. There must be somebody still around that kens the layout of this place and can tell us how to get the acid in."

"I've got a feeling timing is going to be everything on this one."

"Aye, me too, Cap. And it's never been my strong point, as you well know."

"You just keep doing what you're doing, Wiggo," Banks replied. "You're doing a grand job so far."

"Got it," Davies called out. He handed Banks headphones and a hand set. "It's H.Q. in High Holborn. They're a wee bit confused."

"Aye, well they'll just have to get in the queue."

Wiggo listened in to one side of the conversation and caught the gist of the rest while the cap tried to explain to the brass why he was disobeying a fall back order, what he was doing in an old bunker under the embankment and, best of all, what he could possibly want with an old man called George. But the captain could be a tenacious and persuasive wee bugger when he put his mind to it, and ten minutes later he had auld George on the line. Banks handed the headset and mike to Wiggo.

"Your shout, lad. Tell him what we need."

"How are you holding up, auld yin?"

"In need of some liquid refreshment, lad, as

always. What can I do for you?"

"Could you get us the layout of yon bunker you visited in '68? Blueprints would be good. We've found the beastie's lair, and it's in that self-same bunker. Now we want to get a fuckload of acid down here and finish it off."

Even through the headset Wiggo heard the old man suck at his teeth.

"Tricky, even for an old desk warrior like me. Most of everybody I knew who would know is dead and gone. But leave it with me; I'll make some calls. Just don't count on it as your main plan. Getting the thing into an open area where it can all be hosed down at once might be a better option."

"You start thinking about that too then, auld man, and I'll see what I can do at this end. We'll have some stories to tell each other over our next pint."

"I'll hold you to that, youngster," George said, and signed off.

"The game's afoot," Wiggo said as he turned away from the radio.

"In more ways than you know," Davies said. He was standing by the door looking down the long corridor towards the train platform. "We've got incoming."

-WIGGO-

By the time Wiggo rose and joined the others the blob had filled the far end of the corridor, blocking any escape. It oozed forward slowly, picking up the partially eaten bodies in the doorway and passing them backwards down its length as it came.

"I don't have any plan other than burning this fucker," Wiggo said to Banks.

"Then that makes two of us, Sarge. Want first go at it?"

"Don't mind if I do."

Wiggo stepped forward, finger on the trigger, and noted that the protoplasm seemed to shrink away from him, only for a second before coming on again. He was aware of the dangers of blowback in such a confined space so didn't give the thing time to get close. It was still a good twenty yards away down the corridor when he raised the wand and let out a two second wash of flame. Even then he had to stand back as a wall of heat came back at him. When he was able to step forward again he looked down the corridor to see that the blob had retreated, but not all the way and was already gathering again in the doorway. He thought he knew the reason.

"We've got between a ma and her bairns here, lads," he said. "But that gives me an idea. It's risky though."

"Nowt new there then, lad," Banks said. "Let's have it."

"What do you say we let the thing in here with us?"

Banks laughed, then saw that Wiggo was serious.

"Let it in? We'd be stuck here with it and too close to flame it if it attacked."

"There's that, aye. But my hunch is it'll go back through to the nest. It'll protect the bairns."

"And you're willing to bet your life, our lives, on this hunch?"

"It's either that or stand here burning it until we run out of fuel and it gets us anyway? And if we can get it in with the bairns we can kill two blobs with one fire, so to speak."

"You've seen the size of it though. It's bigger now than what'll fit in there; much bigger."

"Aye. But what if, and remember that I'm making this up as I go along, what if it's the original part, the mother part, that comes back. It could be a hive-mind kind of thing. We take out the mother, the rest turns to mush."

Banks laughed.

"You've been watching too many old films, Wiggo. It's rotted your brain."

Wiggo smiled.

"Maybe so, but my gut's still working, and it's telling me I'm on to something. I think we let it in, take what we can get. But I really do think we need to try, for if it gets us and then those spores ripen, then it really is game over for this city."

Banks thought for a minute as they all looked down the corridor. The blob was slowly creeping towards them again.

"Or," Wiggo said, "I could just give it another

wee hot kiss?"

"Fuck it," Banks replied. "I've trusted your gut this far. In for a penny, in for a pound. What do we do?"

"That's the beauty of it, Cap," Wiggo laughed. "We do fuck all. We just stand back and let it do its thing. As long as we keep quiet, I think we'll be fine."

They stood against the wall with their backs to the radio and waited. It felt like an age before the first sign of the thing came through the doorway, a pseudopod no thicker than an axe-handle snaking across the floor. It went straight to the remnants of the glass tank and began to explore the broken glass and twisted metal, slowly climbing up the tank's leg until it was seemingly tasting its way towards the pipe mouth into the brick storeroom beyond. The main body of the thing pushed through the doorway a minute later, one foot, two feet, three feet high off the floor, a glistening, almost transparent tube that gave off the now familiar rainbow aurora.

Wiggo held his breath, finger near the wand trigger, knowing that if they were forced to fire the backwash would almost certainly burn them along with the blob. But it seemed intent on making its way through to the storeroom, ignoring the men as if they were merely part of the furniture.

It kept coming, foot after foot, yard after yard. There were bits embedded in it at irregular intervals, some recognizably human, others mere blobs of semi-molten flesh and hair and clothing, yet more obviously having been rats, pigeons, dogs or cats before all becoming one in the flowing mass of seemingly never-ending protoplasm.

Wiggo was sure that more had already gone in through the pipe than could possibly fit in the chamber beyond and thought they might be forced into firing after all, but just then it showed signs of thinning, a tail end of sorts as the blob tapered away, dragging its whole length into the pipe and leaving behind only a glistening trail or shimmering rainbow aurora.

Wiggo whistled softly and relaxed his grip on the wand. He slowly stepped to the doorway and looked down the corridor; it was clear all the way down to the railway platform outside. He turned to Davies.

"Can you get the auld man on the blower? If he's managed to do anything about the acid, we might have a chance here."

Davies tried the radio but turned back, shaking his head.

"I think we blew a valve and we're not going to get replacement parts for this thing very easily."

At the same time, as if drawn by their voices, protoplasm began to seep back out of the pipe in the tank towards them. Wiggo smiled grimly.

"Ah, bollocks to it. If you want something done, do it yourself. Let's burn this fucker."

-WIGGO-

They went out to stand just beyond the laboratory door, with Banks and Davies at Wiggo's back.

"Back off a bit, lads. That way it'll only be me that's toast if we're too close."

He gave them five seconds; by that time the blob was starting to seep out across the floor of the wrecked tank and he couldn't afford to wait any longer. He took aim with the wand and pulled the trigger. The blob immediately recoiled from the flame, which arced up and along the pipe into the chamber beyond. He kept his finger there for the count of three then released. There was no sign of the blob in the pipe mouth. Without hesitation Wiggo walked forward, climbed up onto the now-smoking remnants of the glass tank and aimed the wand down the pipe.

"This is for Wilkins, fucker," he shouted, and sent another two second burst away into the darkness. He'd been conditioned from years of watching horror movies to expect high piercing screams at this point, but there was only deep silence from beyond, punctuated with the occasional hissing drip of molten protoplasm from the pipe ceiling. He switched on his headlight and sidled into the pipe. Something surged heavily in the shadows ahead. Wiggo took two more steps inside, aimed the wand, and held down the trigger, washing flame into the chamber beyond. Heat came back at him in waves, making the skin tighten on his cheeks and his lips go dry, but he kept his trigger hold tight until the wand sputtered and his tank went empty. Then, instead of backing off he stepped into the storage chamber, moving aside and shouting the others through.

"Get your arses in here. This fucker needs some more time at gas mark five."

Molten residue from the already burned parts of the thing lay in bubbling puddles on the chamber floor, with more of it dripping, like black tar from roof and walls. The bulk of the thing that had so far escaped the flame was built up into a six-foot tall dome over the top of the cluster of spores.

"It's bloody protecting them," Davies said.

"Of course it is. It's their mammy. It's what mammies do," Wiggo replied.

"Well this mother is for burning," Banks said, as he lifted his wand and sent washes of fire over the dome of protoplasm. It sent up thrashing pseudopods in silent frenzy, but it did not budge from the spot, protecting the spores even as it burned. The captain used up half his tank before he stopped. The spores were all that was left in a bubbling, steaming mass of what now looked like black tar.

"Hardy wee fucks, aren't they," Davies said, and stepped forward. By the time he too had used half his tank there was nothing left in the chamber but smoking ooze and a sickly looking, green tinged aurora that was quickly fading.

"Is that it, Sarge?" Davies asked as they backed out into the clearer air of the laboratory.

"We won't know until we can talk to somebody," Wiggo replied. "Are you sure that old radio's fucked?"

"As fucked as a very fucked thing that's just been fucked."

"Then we need to get up out of here, get higher where our radios get a signal. If the job's done, we'll hear soon enough."

Wiggo led them out as they backtracked their way towards the old Aldwych station. He intended to keep backing up until they reached High Holborn, if they hadn't heard anything by then.

The first transmission came through as they were at the foot of the smooth tunnel that would take them all the way up to the Holborn sewer. It wasn't what they wanted to hear.

"We have a fresh sighting," a clipped BBC English voice said in their ears. "Green Park tube station, heading west."

"How large?" another voice said.

The BBC accent slipped with the reply.

"Fucking enormous, sir."

"Bugger," Wiggo said.

They arrived back in High Holborn just in time to get a dressing down from the top brass. Words like 'gross insubordination', 'reduction in rank' and 'jankers for a month' were thrown around and nobody seemed interested in hearing what they'd found in the lab under the embankment. Wiggo looked around for old George but he was nowhere to be seen.

An hour later they were back in their hotel, ordered to get some sleep, for they were going back north in disgrace first thing in the morning, on the Minister's direct order.

-WIGGO-

Wiggo was too wired to even think about sleep. He did what he'd always found best in these kinds of situations; he headed for the bar. The room was in darkness; it was getting on for midnight and the hotel staff had locked up for the night. Wiggo groped along the gantry in the gloom. A voice came from a corner by the window.

"The good stuff's about a foot to your right. Fetch a bottle and a couple of glasses, there's a good lad."

Wiggo did as he was told and returned to the corner. George was there waiting, although about the only thing Wiggo could see was the glow and fade of the tobacco in his pipe as he puffed at it.

"Well, auld yin," he said, pouring them both a large measure of Single Malt, "Looks like we're going home wi' our tails between our legs."

"Speak for yourself, lad," George said, and downed most of his Scotch in one smooth gulp. "I've had the busiest day I've had in years, and we're not done yet. I've come for a favor."

"Did you no' hear? The Minister's shit-canned us."

"That weasel-faced toerag? I knew him when he was still filling his nappies-and that's not as long ago as you might think. He'll toe the line when he's told. They all do when my old department wields the big stick."

Wiggo was starting to adjust to the dark. He saw that George was helping himself to another Scotch.

"So this favor, it's about the beastie?"

"Oh, yes indeed. My lads have come through. We've-requisitioned let's say-the acid tankers and we have a plan of where they might be deployed. There's something we're missing though. Something I thought you might like to be in on."

"And what's that?" Wiggo asked.

"We need someone noisy."

"Aye, we can do that."

"And we need them as bait."

Wiggo reached for the whisky, mainly to give himself time to think.

"Is this all above board and official, like?"

"Yes, well, nearly. As close as MI5 gets when speed is of the essence."

"You were MI5?"

"Still am, in a way. Once in, never out. And my word still has some weight where it matters. Tonight, it mattered. We've been given one shot at this, what our Yank pals call a 'Hail Mary', but with you and I on the job I think we can get it done. Are you in?"

"Me and the other lads?"

"Of course. Can't split a winning team, can we?"

Ten minutes later Wiggo, Banks and Davies were sitting around the table, each with a drink and a smoke in hand, listening to George lay out his plan.

"I think you had the right idea down there in the lab," George said. "But it was the wrong place, not enough room to let the cat see the mouse."

"You have somewhere larger in mind?" Banks asked.

"Not just larger, but iconic. The perfect place to put an enemy of the country to its final rest. We're going to put it down under Nelson's Column."

"What's under there, then?" Wiggo said. "I'm only asking because I always thought there'd be a giant pair of bollocks."

George laughed.

"No, they were put away in storage for safekeeping, at about the same time as the tunnels were dug. When the Jubilee line was getting put in during the Seventies, they had an extra access tunnel built to carry away the debris and provide ventilation. It runs under Trafalgar Square, from the new wing of the National Gallery in the north west down to Charing Cross in the south east. But the thing about it is, it's big, easy to close at both ends, and accessible from above for us to pour in as much acid as we like. All you have to do is get the thing there for us."

"Washing that much hazardous fluid around in a city is a bit risky, is it not?" Banks said.

"Not when you consider the alternative," George answered, knocking back another Scotch that would have floored a horse. "If this doesn't work they're considering incendiaries. The old city has burned too often; I'd rather not see it aflame again."

"Hold your horses, auld yin," Wiggo said. "You skipped over the bit where we just 'get it there.' How do you suggest we do that without getting sucked up for dinner?"

"You know it keys in on sound?"

"Aye."

"Well, there you go then. Get noisy. Do your thing."

And just like that Wiggo had a mental flashback to other Londons; disaster movie Londons, war movie Londons.

"Air raid sirens," he said, and the rest of them looked at him as if he'd gone mad. "No, listen, London still has an active warning system, does it not?"

"It does, yes," George said. "Hasn't been used in donkey's years, but it's kept maintained and ready."

"Can it be isolated? Tweaked such that only Trafalgar Square goes off?"

George smiled.

"I knew I'd come to the right place. Yes, I'm sure it can be done. Just let me make a phone call."

"While you're at it, see if you can get a couple of yon big council trucks that bash newly laid road smooth, you ken the ones? They sound like a cannon going off, and shake the ground like buggery. That should get the beastie's attention."

-WIGGO-

Ten minutes later they were out back of the hotel in the truck getting kitted up. Wiggo picked up a rifle. George took it out of his hands.

"I've got something waiting for us that'll do the job better," he said.

"Flame-thrower?" Wiggo asked, but only got a smile in reply.

The truck made good time down empty streets. Wiggo went up front to look through the front window. It looked like a scene from one of his disaster movies; London lying quiet, newspapers blowing in the wind and nothing moving but them, just another black shadow among many. He had time to smoke a cigarette by a cracked open window then the truck came to a halt in a side street between Leicester Square and the National Gallery.

"All ashore who're going ashore," George said, and went first, leading them to a second truck at the side of the road. "I've got a present for each of you."

The present turned out to be a backpack with an attached pistol-grip wand and trigger. It wasn't a flame-thrower though, and Wiggo was able to take a good guess at the contents.

"Acid wash?"

"Give that boy a coconut," George replied. "Works on compressed air. You should have about a minute's worth of spray each, so use it wisely, and don't get any on you-it's nearly as nasty as the stuff it's meant to kill."

There was a pack for each of them. George pointed down the road to an open manhole.

"This is as close as we can get you. The tunnel we need to get the beast into is fifty yards to the south east; you can't miss it. I'll give you ten minutes to get into position, then the sirens and trucks will kick in and make a racket. After that, it's up to you. You can get me on your helmets on this…" he tapped at an earpiece in his left ear. "Just say when and we start pouring-we've got six different access points covered to ensure equal distribution. Make sure you've got an out first though, okay?"

"We'll see you soon, auld yin," Wiggo replied. "I still owe you a few pints."

They shook hands warmly then Wiggo followed Banks and Davies to the open manhole.

Showtime.

Wiggo checked his watch as they reached the bottom of the ladder into the sewer. Eight minutes to go. If George was right, that was plenty of time for them to reach the mouth of the tunnel. They wouldn't know how best to position themselves until they got there and saw the layout, but Wiggo figured they'd have at least a small gap between making a noise and the thing actually responding to it. The main thing that was worrying him was how they were going to get out before the acid wash turned everything down here to little more than sludge.

Seven minutes to go. They walked in a recently built sewer, concrete rather than brick, but no less smelly than any other they'd been in over the past couple of days. The acid sloshed disconcertingly in the tank on Wiggo's back with every step.

Six minutes to go. They arrived at a junction. To their left and right a wider tunnel stretched away on either side; the one on the left was where George wanted them to herd the blob. Now that they were here Wiggo thought he'd rather be herding kittens. He pointed across the junction to a smaller exit where the sewer kept flowing in that direction.

"I'll take first dibs at standing in the shite, if you lads don't mind," he said. "I deserve it after getting you into this."

He didn't get any disagreement from the others, and walked over to take his place in the sewer mouth. Davies stayed where he was on the other side, while Banks stepped over to watch the right-hand tunnel.

Five minutes to go. Wiggo lit up a smoke, wondering about the dangers of gas build up in confined spaces, and deciding he didn't give a toss. The junction fell quiet, the only sound the occasional splash of running water underfoot.

Four minutes to go. Banks spoke up.

"It's still your shout, Wiggo," he said, "so whatever you want to do, just let us know. Just don't get yourself dead."

"I'll do my best, Cap," he said. "But I cannae promise anything."

Three minutes to go. The tobacco tasted stale in his mouth but at least it kept the worst of the smell at bay. Wiggo looked down the left-hand tunnel and saw it was wide enough to accommodate a full-sized tube train and lit down its length by a line of loosely hung single bulbs that were swaying in a slight breeze. There were ladders at intervals heading up into the square; he guessed these might be what George had called 'access points', places where the acid would rain down once the action got underway. George had also mentioned an 'out' might be possible along the tunnel should it be needed. But the plan was to get the beastie down there, not the squad.

Two minutes to go. Wiggo was getting twitchy. He chewed on the remnants of the smoke then spat it out to hiss away in the running water underfoot. He saw Banks tighten his grip on the trigger of his wand and did the same himself.

One minute. He counted down the seconds in his head. The sirens went off five seconds early, a high wail, only slightly muted here in the tunnels. A few seconds later a rhythmic thumping joined in, like an accompanying bass drum. The thudding appeared to be centered far down the left-hand tunnel, exactly where they wanted the blob to head. George had done his bit to the letter.

"Our turn."

-WIGGO-

They didn't have long to wait.

"Heads up, lads, we've got incoming," Banks said. Wiggo heard it both from across the intersection and in his earpiece. The blob appeared in the wide right-hand tunnel, its presence announced by the immediately recognisable rainbow aurora that preceded it. It filled the tunnel, floor to ceiling, wall to wall, and came forward at a slow walking pace.

"Let it come on," Wiggo said. "If we're lucky there'll be fuck all for us to do but watch."

He should have known it wasn't going to be that simple.

When the front of the protoplasm reached the junction, it stopped and sent out a single pseudopod, a thigh-thick snake that tasted its way around the area, forcing Banks to step back to Davies' side, The pseudopod kept coming, headed directly for Banks and Davies.

"Only hose it down if it gets too close," Wiggo said. "Otherwise, back away and, as George said, let the cat see the mouse."

The tentacle kept heading towards the other two men, who did as Wiggo suggested and backed off. It seemed to sense them somehow and kept following them back up the sewer.

"Bugger this for a game of soldiers," Wiggo said.

He stepped out from his entranceway to stand in

front of the main mass of the blob.

"Hey," he shouted, and stamped his feet. "I'm here. Come and get me, fucker."

The tentacle swung away from the others towards him.

"That's right, fucker, here I am. Breakfast is served."

Wiggo backed away towards the left-hand tunnel mouth, still stamping his feet, splashing in the shallow sewage. In the corner of his eye he saw Banks and Davies step forward, wands raised.

"No, stay back. If this works it'll follow me where we want it to be. You need to hang back, make sure it all comes. This is all or nothing, remember."

"How will you get out?"

"I'm working on it," Wiggo said, still backing away. The pseudopod followed, bringing the mass of the thing out of the tunnel along with it.

Wiggo kept backing up, into the mouth of the tunnel. The blob followed, filling the intersection and cutting him off from the other two men. The die was cast.

End game.

It seemed to take forever. The big bass drums pounded at his back, the air raid sirens wailed and echoed along the whole length of the tunnel and Wiggo kept backing away slowly as the space in front of him filled with the blob and a shimmering aurora almost as bright as the swinging bulbs overhead.

"It's still coming," Banks said in his ear. "How

you doing in there, Sarge?"

"About as well as can be expected for somebody caught in a sealed tube with a moving sausage," Wiggo replied. He tapped at his earpiece. "Are you listening in, auld yin?"

"We're here, lad," George said. "About ten feet above you and twenty feet to your left at a guess. Waiting on your signal."

"Aye? Well haud your horses for a bit. I haven't got an out yet and won't until this fucker's ready for its bath."

He passed a ladder on his right and risked a look up, saw dim light up there above a grate. It was an out, of sorts, but not one he could chance to take, not while there was still some of the protoplasm back out in the tunnels. He kept backing away, kept stamping his feet and shouting oaths at the thing.

It kept coming forward.

He was more than halfway down the tunnel towards the blocked off entrance when Banks spoke in his ear.

"Looks like we're near the arse end," the captain said. "It's thinning out. A couple of extra bits came in from the sewer and merged with it too. With luck the gang's all here."

"Our cunning plan is working," Wiggo said, and had to step back faster as the blob sent a pseudopod snaking in his direction. "Wait till it's nearly all in, then give it a skoosh up the backside, see if you can force it deeper into this tunnel."

"And what about you, Sarge?"

Wiggo cast a glance over his shoulder. He wasn't

that far off from coming up against the sealed wall at the southern end. There was only one more ladder visible, about six feet this side of the end.

"I might have an out," he said. "George? Does the last ladder lead anywhere?"

"Yes," the old man came back. "But it's sealed at the top. You'll have to give us a few minutes to get to it."

At the same time Banks came back on the air.

"That's the last of it, Sarge, but it's looking like it might be starting to back out again."

"We can't have that, can we," Wiggo said. "Give it a fright. And George... you'd better get somebody moving, for I'll be coming up fast. Get ready to let rip."

Wiggo turned and made a dash for the end of the corridor, yelling as he went.

"Last call for breakfast, fucker. Come and get it."

The blob surged forward, whether because it was making a dash for Wiggo or because Banks and Davies had just given it a jolt in the arse, Wiggo didn't care. He reached the ladder and started to climb. The blob was already almost at his feet.

"Hose it down. Do it now," Wiggo yelled.

"But you're not free," George said.

"Fuck that. I'm climbing, and it's following me. Hose it, it's our last chance."

Wiggo concentrated on heading upward. Somewhere in the distance he heard a rush as of running water, and seconds later smelled an acrid, vinegar-like tang. The protoplasm below began to bubble and hiss. But it continued to pile up below him, getting closer to his feet.

The ladder ascended into a closed tube above the tunnel. By the time he reached it the plasm was lapping at his heels, bubbling as if boiling, but filling the tube below him as he kept pulling himself upward. He chanced a look up but saw only darkness above.

"If I take my last breath on this fucking ladder, there'll be hell to pay," Wiggo said. Nobody answered and when he tapped his earpiece he got only static.

"Bugger."

He climbed. The frothing protoplasm climbed with him. He put all his effort into it, arms and calves feeling the burn, the acid sloshing in the tank at his back. The air grew thick and warm, the tang of vinegar almost overpowering. He pulled up, one last effort and there was a clang as his helmet met metal; a submarine-style hatchway. He turned the handle above him and pushed. Nothing gave. The bloody thing was locked.

Below him the plasm seethed and roiled. He got himself turned, pointed the wand down and pulled the trigger. A wash of acid brought tears to his eyes. Through blurred vision he saw the plasm retreat six feet down the tube then almost immediately start back up, as if propelled by a greater mass below.

"Fuck off and die, you bastard thing," Wiggo shouted, and washed it again.

It retreated once more, then came back even faster.

"Where the fuck are you, auld yin? Get me out of here."

The plasm lapped at his feet. He sent another

wash of acid down onto it, splashing his boots. He smelled burning rubber as the soles melted. There was a spluttering sound, and a hiss as the tank ran empty.

The plasm was still bubbling and roiling three feet below his feet, sending up noxious clouds of vinegar-laced vapor.

"Die, you bastard. Just fucking die," Wiggo whispered.

A pseudopod snaked up, heading for Wiggo's ankles. He had nothing with which to defend himself.

There was a clang, and sudden light from above.

"Move your head to the left a bit, there's a good lad," George said, and when Wiggo complied the old man sent a wash of acid down the tube to splash over the pseudopod.

When Wiggo looked down he saw the plasm, boiling furiously, retreat into the dark.

They waited for long seconds.

It didn't come back.

-WIGGO-

Wiggo climbed out to join George in the open air. A hazy dawn was rising over Trafalgar Square. They were standing some six feet above it on a plinth, between the paws of a great lion. The paved stones of the square ran with smoking acid and noxious, rainbow infused smoke rose up from grates and manholes. Off to their left two tankers were still pouring acid down to the depths below.

"Will we get it all?" Wiggo asked.

"I'd hope so," George replied. "But if not, we know how to deal with it now, and the lads in the office no longer think I'm a crazy old sod. They'll take it seriously."

Wiggo looked across the square and saw Banks and Davies up on the National Gallery steps, giving him a thumbs-up. A pigeon flew in from the Buckingham Palace direction, landed on the lion's head and promptly shat on it.

"Normality returns," George said. He clapped Wiggo on the back. "Now lad, about those pints you owe me?"

Check out other great

Cryptid Novels!

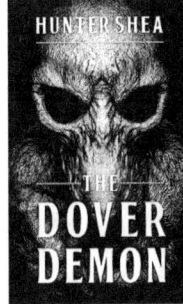

Hunter Shea

THE DOVER DEMON

The Dover Demon is real...and it has returned. In 1977, Sam Brogna and his friends came upon a terrifying, alien creature on a deserted country road. What they witnessed was so bizarre, so chilling, they swore their silence. But their lives were changed forever. Decades later, the town of Dover has been hit by a massive blizzard. Sam's son, Nicky, is drawn to search for the infamous cryptid, only to disappear into the bowels of a secret underground lair. The Dover Demon is far deadlier than anyone could have believed. And there are many of them. Can Sam and his reunited friends rescue Nicky and battle a race of creatures so powerful, so sinister, that history itself has been shaped by their secretive presence? "THE DOVER DEMON is Shea's most delightful and insidiously terrifying monster yet." – Shotgun Logic Reviews "An excellent horror novel and a strong standout in the UFO and cryptid subgenres." –Hellnotes "Non-stop action awaits those brave enough to dive into the small town of Dover, and if you're lucky, you won't see the Demon himself!" – The Scary Reviews PRAISE FOR SWAMP MONSTER MASSACRE "B-horror movie fans rejoice, Hunter Shea is here to bring you the ultimate tale of terror!" – Horror Novel Reviews "A nonstop thrill ride! I couldn't put this book down." – Cedar Hollow Horror Reviews

Armand Rosamilia

THE BEAST

The end of summer, 1986. With only a few days left until the new school year, twins Jeremy and Jack Schaffer are on very different paths. Jeremy is the geek, playing Dungeons & Dragons with friends Kathleen and Randy, while Jack is the jock, getting into trouble with his buddies. And then everything changes when neighbor Mister Higgins is killed by a wild animal in his yard. Was it a bear? There's something big lurking in the woods behind their New Jersey home.Will the police be able to solve the murder before more Middletown residents are ripped apart?

Check out other great

Cryptid Novels!

Edward J. McFadden III

THE CRYPTID CLUB

When cryptozoologist Ash Cohn receives a gold embossed printed invitation inviting him to join The Cryptid Club, he sees the resolution to all his problems.Famous cryptid scientist and biologist, Lester Treemont, one of the world's richest men, and the leader of the Cryptid Club, is dying. What he offers via his invitation is a chance to succeed him. To take over his wealth, laboratory, and discoveries. All Ash has to do is beat eight others like him in a series of tests both mental and physical involving Treemont's collection of cryptids. Seems simple enough, and Ash has nothing to lose.Nine strangers from across the globe, all with reasons for wanting to win. When they start dying one by one, the competition shifts to one of survival. Who among them will rise to the top and reign over The Cryptid Club?

William Meikle

INFESTATION

It was supposed to be a simple mission. A suspected Russian spy boat is in trouble in Canadian waters. Investigate and report are the orders. But when Captain John Banks and his squad arrive, it is to find an empty vessel, and a scene of bloody mayhem. Soon they are in a fight for their lives, for there are things in the icy seas off Baffin Island, scuttling, hungry things with a taste for human flesh. They are swarming. And they are growing. "Scotland's best Horror writer" - Ginger Nuts of Horror "The premier storyteller of our time." - Famous Monsters of Filmland

Check out other great

Cryptid Novels!

Ian Faulkner

CRYPTID

Be careful what you look for. You might just find it.1996. A group of 14 students walked into the trackless virgin forests of Graham Island, British Columbia for a three-day hike. They were never seen again. 2019. An American TV crew retrace those students' steps to attempt to solve a 23-year-old mystery. A disparate collection of characters arrives on the island. But all is not as it seems. Two of them carry dark secrets. Terrible knowledge that will mean death for some – but a fighting chance of survival for others. In the hidden depths of the forests – man is on the menu. Some mysteries should remain unsolved...

Eric S. Brown

LOCH NESS HORROR

The Order of the Eternal Light, a secret organization have foretold the end of the human race. In order to save all humanity, agents of the Order must locate the Loch Ness Monster and obtain a sample of its blood for within in it is the key to stopping the apocalypse but finding the monster will be no easy task.

www.ingramcontent.com/pod-product-compliance
Lightning Source LLC
Chambersburg PA
CBHW061251170626
46809CB00007B/2938